BERRY BETRAYAL

A SMALL TOWN CULINARY COZY MYSTERY

THE COZY CAFÉ MYSTERIES

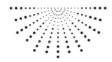

BOOK FOUR

C. A. PHIPPS

Cozy Café Mysteries

DEDICATION

For my husband, who makes my life better every day.

Cheryl 🩶

BERRY BETRAYAL

Something scary has come to Cozy Hollow!

Tasked with cataloging an important citizen's family treasures, Violet Finch is finally following her dreams of assessing antiques and books—until items go missing.

Her mentor's training ensures that Violet can't help being intrigued by the surrounding mystery. However, she's also worried that her eldest sister Scarlett won't manage the Cozy Café without her once she qualifies and leaves town.

While the rest of the family intends to smooth the transition, things soon turn pear-shaped when a friend is murdered. If her guess over the thief's identity is correct, she might not be hunting more than one criminal. The sheriff is unimpressed with her half-baked ideas, or how the clues find her first, but rescue pets, Bob and George, seem to think she's on the right track.

Can Violet, her sisters, and the pets, solve the crimes? Or have they become the new targets?

The Cozy Café mysteries are light cozy mysteries featuring family-focused café owners who discover they're talented amateur sleuths—and a magnet for animals.

Other books in the series:
Book 1 Sweet Saboteur
Book 2 Candy Corruption
Book 3 Mocha Mayhem
Book 4 Berry Betrayal
Enjoy a FREE recipe or two in every book!

CHAPTER ONE

The coffee machine burst into life as Violet made a takeout coffee for Deputy Glasson. She smiled the way she'd been taught and took his money, while inside she groaned for the hundredth time—and it wasn't even lunchtime.

Some things weren't meant to be and several years ago Violet developed the distinct impression her career was one of those things. It wasn't a case of self-pity—mostly. Just the feeling of being in limbo around a desired career, one she was desperate to embark on, as opposed to the job of baking.

She'd made inroads to reaching her goal, and now she was impatient for it to begin. Some (her sisters) might say she was born impatient. And they wouldn't be completely wrong.

To be fair, running the family café with her two sisters wasn't the worst thing to do—if she didn't have plans. Now that baby-sister Ruby had her dream job as the full-time librarian, she had little time to help. This meant it fell to Violet who didn't consider herself a true baker, to assist their eldest sister. Scarlett was adamant about keeping the café alive and would be miserable if it closed. Since Violet didn't want that on her shoulders for the rest of her life she promised to stay until qualifying as an assessor of antiques.

"Any chance of a refill?" Leona Wolf held up her cup and wiggled it like she was changing a lightbulb.

Violet came out of her reverie with a start. Why was she feeling so down today, when her training was already underway in a theoretical capacity and about to begin in earnest practically? It made no sense. Unless she took into account that she would be leaving Scarlett to deal with everything on her own. Guilt certainly played a part in her mood, and she wasn't sure how to quieten the negative voice inside her head. With her sisters' blessings to pursue her career, she was determined to take the opportunity. Still...

"Sorry, here you go." Violet filled the now stable cup. "Anyone else?"

The craft group was at full quota today. The four stalwarts were always interested in the Finch sisters and unfortunately no questions were deemed inappropriate.

"Yes, please." Linda Night smiled kindly. "Are you still off next month for your new job?"

"Yes, but my training begins this weekend. Will you miss me?" she joked.

"Well, I'm sure we will a little bit," Leona told her matter-of-factly. "Probably not as much as if it were Ruby. She's such a sweetie."

Violet snorted at the backhanded compliment. "Unlike me?"

"Oh dear, have I said the wrong thing? I only meant you're not really cut out for being a server."

"She's not just a server, Mrs. Wolf." Scarlett placed a large berry muffin in front of the matronly figure with more force than necessary. "Violet is a great baker too."

"I'm sure she is, but sadly not as good as you or your mom."

Knowing it would do no good, yet pleased by her sister defending her, Violet shook her head at Scarlett to stop her from arguing the case. "Now that I'm suitably pigeonholed as the least talented, excuse me ladies. I have dishes to wash and floors to scrub. A bit like Cinderella." She stopped on her way back to the kitchen to place the coffee pot on its stand, wondering how that had gone down and suspected the comment went over their heads.

Scarlett followed and placed a hand gently on her shoulder, giving it a squeeze. "Don't listen to Mrs. Wolf. She doesn't think before she speaks and I'm sure isn't intentionally trying to be unkind."

"Maybe not, but we both know it sums up in a nutshell what the town thinks of me."

"That's just silly, Vi. The people who feel like that don't know you the way the rest of us do."

Violet put a hand over her sister's and squeezed it back. "Thanks, but you know I don't need anyone else's approval and I'm not going to lose sleep over it."

Scarlett gave her a skeptical look. "That's the spirit. Have you heard from Phin?"

Violet couldn't stop the grin at the mention of her mentor, a renowned assessor who had taken her under his wing. "He phoned first thing this morning. The training is all set up in Destiny, which means I can commute for most of it and won't have to pay for accommodation. Lucky for me he has a lot of work there for the next few months."

"It couldn't have worked out better for you." Scarlett sounded sincere.

"It will mean taking one of the cars though."

"Don't you worry about that. Ruby and I can carpool and I'm sure Aunt Olivia will help if necessary."

"Is she any further along with selling the craft store?"

"According to Olivia, it sounds like it's pretty close to being sorted and the group informed me that they have appointments with banks and lawyers."

"Thank goodness for that. I know you're anxious about not having me around."

"I'll absolutely miss you, but we made this decision a long time ago and no matter what, I won't renege on my side of it. The café is doing well enough that if I have to do reduced hours and not have as many items on sale, then that's perfectly fine and nothing for you to worry about. Ruby will help in the mornings and Gail Norman will watch the craft store over lunch so Olivia can help then."

Scarlett made it sound as if things were sorted, but Violet knew how hard she worked already. Without Violet, Scarlett would be lucky to get a break all day and would have to handle the breakfast rush when Ruby left to open the library.

The bell over the door jangled, breaking into another downward spiral and the mayor strolled in.

"How are we ladies?" Arthur Tully gave a small bow to the craft group and fielded a few questions about town happenings before making his escape to the counter. "Some days getting away is easier than others." He winked to take the sting out of his words.

Violet chuckled. "Tell me about it."

Scarlett tutted at both of them. "What can we do for you today, Mayor?"

"I'd like one of your pasties and a coffee to go, please."

The pasties were an English take on a meat pie. Flakey pastry was folded over in an oval shape and contained rich gravy, beef and vegetables. She bagged the order, while Violet made the coffee, both happy to chat with their once enemy and now firm friend.

Arthur leaned around the machine so he could see Violet. "Do you have a minute to spare for a chat anytime soon?"

His hushed tone and intense look intrigued her. "Sure. The group has their food and coffee and we're not busy right now if it's urgent."

He glanced behind him. "Not here. I'd like to discuss something in private."

Now she was really interested. "I do have to pick up a few things from the stationers. Shall I come to your office?"

He chewed his top lip for a moment. "I'd rather not. There are too many people hanging around there lately."

"Okay." Violet was confused and Scarlett who caught the tail end of the conversation had a frown so deep Violet was worried it might become permanent. "What do you suggest?"

"Have we done something wrong?" Scarlett blurted before he could answer. "You're scaring us a little."

Violet stiffened, remembering how he had been so against them and the café not so long ago, but he laughed. Only, it wasn't the sort of laugh that made you want to join in which was almost worse than his seriousness.

"I have a little problem that I think Violet could help me out with. I just don't want all the busybodies knowing about it."

Violet raised an eyebrow. "If you can tell me who doesn't fall into that category, we might be able to avoid them."

This time he laughed properly. "I'm being dramatic, but it is a sensitive issue."

"Why don't you two go into the kitchen," Scarlett suggested with a look at Violet that said she would expect all the details.

Arthur licked his lips nervously once more and Violet's curiosity went next level. "Come on, before the lunch rush hits."

He followed her and she offered him a chair at the

scrubbed table in the center of the room. As soon as she sat opposite he toyed with the bag and his takeaway coffee cup. Arthur was not a fidgety kind of man, and she waited impatiently for him to spit out whatever was bothering him.

He coughed. "The thing is, I know you're not qualified, but I need you to look at an antique I have and tell me if it's authentic."

She let out the breath she'd been holding. "Is that all? You're right I'm not qualified and won't be for some time. Whatever I could tell you about it would be pure guess work."

"You've spent a lot of time with that assessor," he scoffed. "And you're a smart cookie, so I daresay some of the training has already rubbed off. Plus, you discovered the truth about that book your mom had hidden away for years. Which proves you have talent. Could you just take a look, so I know if I'm going crazy or not?"

Arthur looked so desperate that Violet didn't correct him, even though it was Scarlett who pushed the investigation in the right way to solve the mystery of the missing family heirloom several months ago. Besides, her curiosity had quadrupled. "I guess it couldn't hurt to look, as long as you understand that what I say isn't definitive. I don't want to mislead you in any way."

He closed his eyes for a second and sighed. "I accept that and thank you for helping."

"Don't thank me yet. What do you mean about whether it's authentic or not? You sound like you're suggesting it once was and now you're not sure."

"That's exactly what I mean. I think it's recently been switched for a forgery right under my nose. The item has been in my family for a long time, and I look at it every day. Something's been bugging me about it for a few days, but I've been a bit stressed and brushed it off. However, this morning I took a closer look and realized that it really is different."

"In what way?"

"I'd rather you saw it first before I say more—if you don't mind."

The intrigue made her fingers itch to touch the object. "Actually, that makes sense, then I won't be looking for your point of difference."

He nodded enthusiastically. "Exactly. When can you come?"

"After work?"

"Perfect. I'll be home, so just come right in."

There was no mistaking the slight shake in his voice and that was telling. Whatever was happening, regardless of it being theft or his imagination, clearly upset him. Always a staunch man, unafraid to tackle anyone who crossed him, when it came to private matters she imagined that asking for help didn't come easy.

After the ugliness of his relationship to the Finch sisters came out into the open, and Arthur finally accepted the infatuation with their mom was exacerbated by PTSD, he'd gotten the right help he desperately needed. Once the right medication kicked in, Arthur became incredibly kind and ridiculously generous as if to make amends for the heartache he'd caused by wanting them to leave town. It would be nice if she could repay some of that later kindness by easing his mind. Yet, it was a little nerve wracking when she considered this would be her first solo act as an assessor. *An unqualified assessor,* she reminded herself.

It wouldn't do to get ahead of the game and make a fool of herself by showing off what she thought she knew—and fall flat on her face.

CHAPTER TWO

As soon as they'd closed and cleaned the café, Violet dropped Scarlett at their home, a couple of miles away, then headed back to the mayor's house which was in town. The old Victorian had seen better days, but she knew that Arthur was doing renovations inside. Pulling the car into the driveway she appreciated the gables and bay windows. It must have been a stunner at one time, and would be once more.

At the oak door, she let the large brass ring drop with a resounding clang and turned to admire the gardens at the front, which were a mass of wildflowers. It seemed Arthur had a new gardener.

After what seemed an age, she used the brass knocker again and waited. The front veranda was swept clean, and clematis clung to the trellis at both ends. The riot of white blooms with magenta speckles hid the peeling facade, and the smell wafted over her from several feet away. The hedges of camellias in pink, red, orange, and yellow, made her smile. When Violet and her sisters admired them, Arthur took clippings and helped transplant them around the Finch house.

Their mayor liked things neat and, in the past, had made derogatory remarks about the state of the Finch house. To be fair, his illness and bad temper aside, he'd been right. After their mom died, money had been worse than tight, but the house had been slipping into decline long before that. With a good deal of community spirit, the old house was looking pretty good these days. Maybe she should offer to get a working bee together to paint Arthur's house.

She chuckled at the idea of turning up to a working bee as they had for the Finch's. Arthur wasn't the type to ask for help and liked his privacy.

Yet, he had asked her to stop by. So, where was he? Maybe he'd gotten so busy he forgot about it. Whatever the reason she couldn't stand out here all night. Then she remembered, he'd said to come right in.

Cozy Hollow was an old-fashioned town and people didn't generally walk in unannounced, but there was no telling how long she might wait otherwise. Gingerly turning the handle, she had to use a bit of force to push the door open. It creaked a little and then she was standing in a wide hall. An ornate coat rack stood to her left; the rest of the space was empty.

"Something's missing," she muttered. "Hello, Arthur? It's me, Violet Finch."

There was a thud from somewhere, then an eerie silence descended. Not known for being a scaredy-cat, and despite her heart thumping, she moved slowly past the rather grand staircase toward the back of the house. The doors on either side of the hall were shut. She thought the bedrooms were upstairs, but wasn't absolutely certain that there wasn't one on this floor, and wouldn't like to barge in on him unannounced if he was resting.

She'd been inside the house a few times with her mom before Lilac got sick, however they'd always sat in the conservatory attached to the dining room, which overlooked the back yard. Maybe she should have come via the back door instead.

"Hello?" It didn't feel right to wander through his house, but it was too late to backtrack now, and what if he'd hurt himself and was laying injured?

A head peeked around the last door at the far end. "Oh, it's just you."

Violet shrieked. "Sheesh! You frightened the life out of me."

The rest of him appeared and he shrugged. "Sorry. I did say come in."

"Next time, you might say it louder," she fumed, her heart taking its sweet time to get back to normal.

"I had my head in a trunk, so I guess my voice was muffled."

He did look apologetic, and since it was her imagination going off on a mystery tangent which was mostly to blame, she shook off her annoyance. "Never mind. I'm here now, so what do you want to talk about?"

"In here." He ushered her into a study where every wall was lined with books. A heavy oak desk took pride of place almost in the middle of the room, and though the curtains were drawn, a gorgeous lamp on one end of the desk sparkled rainbow colors across a decent area. A large leather edged blotter sat underneath a laptop, with an ornate pen and ink well in front of them. She sighed. "This is an exquisite room. I don't think I've ever been in here."

He looked around the room with mild surprise, then smiled proudly. "This was my father's and grandfather's study. It is a nice, comfortable room."

"Nice?" She scoffed. "It's way beyond that. I'd kill for a room like this, and I bet Ruby would too."

His fondness for Ruby was no secret, and the smile

widened. Because of his feelings for their mom and with Ruby an almost exact replica, she had a special place in his heart. A heart that at one time had been shriveled and full of open dislike, had softened and expanded to include Violet and Scarlett.

"I offered her the use of my library whenever she likes, but so far she hasn't taken me up on it." A little sadness tinged his voice.

This was not the same man who had tried to run them out of town. Which was the most amazing turn-around she'd ever witnessed, and her heart ached a little for him. "I'm sure she will when she finds time. Running the library and helping out on weekends and mornings at the café keep her busy."

He smiled again. "Yes, of course. She's as dedicated to her work as she is to the café—you all are."

She gave an awkward nod. "I don't mean to be rude, but I do have studying to catch up on."

"Of course, and I don't want to keep you. Come over here." He beckoned her nearer and swallowed as if his throat hurt. "I have some treasures from my family that I dot around the house, and I've noticed that they are disappearing."

This did not sound good and now the near empty hall made sense. "Have you told the sheriff?"

"I have. Nate is looking into things." His eyes clouded. "So, he says. Personally, I think he's handed over the case to his new deputy who seems a bit wet behind the ears."

Violet wouldn't let him bad-mouth Nate, who was a friend—and in Scarlett's case, possibly more than that. "Nate's a good sheriff. If he told you he's doing his job, then you should trust him. And if he has faith in his deputy, then surely you could give the man the benefit of the doubt."

"Hmmmph. I guess you're right. Deputy Pine seems nice

enough, but he didn't seem to do anything other than ask a lot of questions. The truth is, I need some action on this before I do go crazy."

He sounded desperate, which wasn't like Arthur at all. "So, these disappearing items aren't a new thing?"

"Not at all." He sighed deeply. "It started about a month ago and I find something missing every few days."

If this were true, and she had no real reason to doubt the mayor, then the person responsible wasn't worried about the sheriff catching them. "Are you sure the items aren't, ah, simply moved."

"You mean, am I going senile and misplacing or losing things that have sat in the same place since before I was born?" Arthur suggested dryly.

When he put it like that it seemed unlikely, but Arthur had received a head injury and had done things the doctors didn't hold him responsible for before this. Still, she didn't want to dredge that up when he was clearly upset. The need to tread gently seemed appropriate. "Stranger things have happened in Cozy Hollow."

Surprisingly, he snorted. "Good point. In fact, I had a terrible thought that maybe I *was* going crazy, so I started taking photos of the more valuable items as proof—for the sheriff's and my benefit."

"That was a clever idea. Did the photos prove you were right?"

He nodded. "They did. I must admit I was relieved, but that was short term because like I say, things keep disappearing. A couple of days ago I'd had enough and decided to lock a few things in this trunk."

He pointed to behind his desk where the lid was hanging from the back of the biggest trunk she had ever seen.

"You're kidding me!" She rushed around the desk, her fingers itching to touch the beautiful piece of luggage. "This is amazing. Look at the handcrafted detail on the wood and the leather."

"It was my grandfather's war chest," he said proudly.

"I've always pitied the poor men and horses who had to get the officers trunks from A to B in awful weather and road conditions."

He nodded again. "And it survived everything you can imagine. So, you'd think that as sturdy as it is, and with me having the only key in my pocket, it would be as good as a safe."

Her jaw slacked for a moment. "And it isn't?"

Arthur's whole face drooped. "Unfortunately, it gave up its contents as soon as my back was turned."

When she frowned at the odd comment he shrugged. "I'm not sleeping well and so I began coming downstairs to check on things. I couldn't believe it when I realized that my diligence did nothing to deter the thief."

Violet shuddered at the idea of someone walking around as bold as brass, not caring that the owner was upstairs and could appear at any moment. Plus, Arthur could have been hurt if he'd confronted the guilty party.

She shook off the visuals her imagination delivered and peered inside the chest. There were several books, a saber, a very old watch, and some medals. "Arthur, if you have the sheriff involved, and there are pieces missing, what exactly do you want from me?"

He coughed and opened his hand. "Like I said in the café, I want your expertise. This was given to me by my father. I need to know if it's real."

Despite her misgivings about his use of the word expertise, Violet couldn't help the thrum of excitement that coursed through her at the sight of a precious possession. Holding out her hand toward him, Arthur gently let a ring slide onto it. She cupped her hand and raised it to her face. "This is beautifully made."

"But is it real or a fake?"

He was so close his breath sighed against her cheek and the irony of another crime involving old rings wasn't lost on her. "I can't say for sure. There are tests for that sort of thing, but none I have the tools for yet. What do you know about it?"

"It was my grandfathers'. He got it when he graduated from engineering school after the army. My father was also an engineer, and his ring is missing."

His face told her how sad this made him, and she took a minute to search her memory. "I do know that receiving pinkie rings is a thing in either engineering or ecology when you graduate. You must be very proud of both of them."

He rubbed his finger absently. "I am which makes this whole business so upsetting and infuriating."

"I can imagine. What I don't understand is why you think a person would steal some things but swap this ring for a fake."

"I know it sounds weird, but a couple of times the items were returned as if the thief thought I wouldn't know the original." He huffed. "I know everything in this house. At least I used to. Now I'm not sure."

"Because?"

"This ring had a small dent underneath the top. It used to rub the base of my finger, so I stopped wearing it years ago, meaning to get it fixed."

Violet turned the ring over and felt the smoothness of the gold. "No dent. You can't imagine something that causes acute physical discomfort, so I guess we can rule out the crazy."

"I'm not sure our sheriff is as convinced." Arthur pursed his lips. "Even with photographic evidence."

Violet wasn't about to get into that. "I'm going to see Phin on the weekend to get more paperwork for my course and have some lessons prior to my first exams. I could take it with me and get him to test it."

He took the ring from her and held it a moment before pulling a small cloth bag from the trunk. He placed it gently inside and tied the purse strings before handing it to her. "I'd appreciate your help. Please look after it."

She gulped at the fear in his eyes. *No pressure.* "I'll do my best and I hope you find the thief soon."

"Me too. It's very unnerving to think a stranger is coming in here and rifling through my stuff, picking out the choice bits of my family history."

He saw her to the door, and she heard it lock behind her. Hopefully Phin would be able to give him the answer he craved. Arthur was desperate for answers and Phin was so good at his job, therefore she was positive they would find answers to the missing and/or swapped items.

CHAPTER THREE

Scarlett had brought home one of the family pies from the café and was dishing up the meal when Violet got home. Any arrival wasn't as simple as coming in and washing up. Not when Bob hadn't seen her all day. He bounced around her like a kangaroo looking for treats which included, but wasn't limited to, pats and compliments.

"Hello, Bob. Who's a good boy!"

He flung himself across the doorway so she had to bend and pat him before she could get inside. Unfortunately, their large tabby had been washing himself in that exact spot. George swatted the lab, and Bob, incapable of taking the hint, licked the cat across his face. The cat complained loudly and strutted off to a safer place.

"Oh Bob, you're a fool," she crooned. Annoying George was his favorite thing to do, and he didn't care about the consequences, which made him a star in her eyes. She loved George, but he was the bossiest cat in the world and needed taking down a peg or two from time to time. Or maybe she was simply giving Bob too much credit.

"Hurry up, we're dying to know what the mayor wanted," Ruby called from where she finished setting the table.

"What if it's a secret?" Violet teased, removing her shoes with a grateful sigh.

Ruby grinned mischievously. "Even better."

"Hah! I guess I can tell you if you'll keep it to yourselves."

"Don't we always? No don't answer that," Scarlett added.

"Give me a minute to wash up." Violet left them to their groans but did hurry and when they were finally all seated, shared the story. "I think that's everything."

Scarlett got that far-away look when she was working through everything, and the others ate silently to give her time. She had such a clever mind when it came to motives and tying in clues that her sisters were in awe watching the process.

A little while later, Violet ran out of patience. "Nice pie," she commented, hoping to bring Scarlett back to them.

Ruby pointed her fork. "Didn't you make it?"

"What's your point?" Violet challenged. "It's still nice, right?"

"True, and it goes well with the vegetable medley I made."

"It does and the pie is only marginally better." Not a vegetable lover, Violet knew that Ruby had done her best to make it tasty so she would eat it, but teasing each other was ingrained in them as much as their protectiveness.

Ruby poked out her tongue. "You're so competitive!"

"Both dishes are lovely." Scarlett sighed. "Mom would be proud of the skill and team work."

As usual, any mention of their mom stopped all bickering, even that which was done in fun.

Violet coughed to get her sister's attention. "Back to the mayor's dilemma. If someone got into the house and the trunk without breaking in, then they have access."

Scarlett lined up the condiments in front of her. "You think the thief is a member of his staff?"

"Very likely." Violet had considered this on the drive home. "Or it could be someone else who knows where he keeps his keys. Which implies they have access to him because the trunk key is in his pocket—I'm assuming most of the time."

"He wouldn't sleep with it in his pocket, would he?"

"Good point, Ruby. Unless his jammies have a wee pocket. Perhaps he tucks it under his pillow."

"I didn't know the tooth fairy liked brass," Ruby chuckled.

"Hahaha. He'd have to be a sound sleeper, to not feel a key digging into his skin, and the thief would need to get inside the house first."

"Which clearly isn't an issue," Scarlett mused.

Violet nodded. "We could ask him who works there now, or did in the past, who had the keys at any time."

"I think you'll find that's the sheriff's job," Scarlett said firmly

"And when has that ever stopped you?" Violet demanded.

"That was in my reckless days." Scarlett sniffed. "I'm a changed woman."

"Since when? The last case we cracked was barely three months ago."

Shuddering, Scarlett shook her head. "That was a horrible time in our lives. I don't want to ever be in that position again."

"Speaking of positions. How are you and the sheriff getting on?" Ruby asked innocently.

Scarlett blinked and then shrugged. "I'm not sure. One moment he's ready to date and the next minute he's a little cool."

Ruby made a soothing noise. "I think he's worried you still have a thing for Sam."

Scarlett had been enamored with the paramedic, until she found out he was in love with another woman—one he couldn't have. Violet was proud of the way Scarlett had dealt with being his second best and Sam was no longer on her friend list.

"Well, I don't." Scarlett huffed.

Ruby gave her the side-eye. "Are you sure?"

"I don't know what to say to him, so I avoid Sam like the plague."

"Which is not really the same thing," Violet ventured.

"In this case it is. I'm embarrassed that I didn't see the truth, and annoyed at myself for wanting to settle for something that was easy. It took a while, but I realized that I wanted a relationship and Sam seemed ideal. That's nothing like real love, is it?"

Violet and Ruby shared a look. Scarlett did not reveal her inner self very often, so explaining how she felt about the doomed relationship was a huge milestone. The way she said it with such honesty meant what she said was the truth, and that she trusted them to believe her.

"Do you hate Sam for what he did?" Ruby asked gently.

"How can I? Maybe I was angry for a while, but he's a good guy who did something stupid because the love of his life was marrying someone else. He didn't mean to hurt me. I guess he wanted someone too—and unfortunately for me, I fitted the bill."

Since they were being so open about things, Violet couldn't hold back. "But what if you hadn't found that out until it was too late, and you got married?"

"There's no point in worrying about it, because I did find out." Scarlett stood and began clearing the table. "Now, can we please move on and stop harping about it?"

Violet shrugged. "I didn't realize we were. It's more a case of making sure you're all right and not simply putting on a brave face."

Scarlett looked like she would argue, then she shook her head and gave them a bright smile. "I know and appreciate that it's good to talk about things, but I feel this subject's been talked to death. We can't change a thing that happened. I need to move on and not give it any more time. We all do."

"Okay, point taken." Violet turned to Ruby. "So how are you getting on with the giant?"

Ruby giggled. "Great. Alex came to the library this afternoon and showed me his plans."

"Marriage plans?" Violet waggled her eyebrows.

"Stop it." Ruby screwed up her cute button nose. "We're just friends and you know I meant the plans for refurbishing the diner."

"Hmmm. Are you sure about the friends tag? The way he looks at you reminds me of the wolf and little red riding hood."

Pink-cheeked, Ruby waved away the idea. "You're being ridiculous again."

"You agree with me Scarlett, right?" Violet persisted.

"Leave me out of it. I like Alex, but clearly I have no idea about men, so I'll simply wish you both luck for when you're ready to date."

Violet snorted. "Yeah, well don't either of you hold your breath on my account."

They eyed each other warily. It was fair to say none of them had a good track record when it came to the men in their lives and while they did want each other to be happy, it was easier to see the mistakes the others made rather than their own.

"I'm happy with the way my life is right now." Ruby was the first to break the impasse.

"Me too." Scarlett nodded. "Who needs the complication?"

Violet grimaced. "Agreed, and I think dessert will make me happier still."

The conversation had been diverted once again from the mayor's property being stolen and while it had been interesting to learn how her sisters' love lives were doing, Violet was eager to get her hands on that ring with Phin and do some testing for real.

Her hand went to her pocket, and she snickered softly at the idea of copying Bilbo Baggins and his precious. Although, in her case, this wasn't about obsession, it was about her dream coming true and if she could help someone along the way it would be a double blessing.

Bob barked a warning making them jump and George marched to the back door before a shadow appeared outside.

With a shifty look, Ruby headed across the kitchen. "By the way, Alex is stopping by to show me the alterations he's making based on my earlier suggestions for the diner."

"You sneaky…evening Alex." Violet chuckled.

Surprised by her reaction he wiped his face with a large hand as if worried it might be dirty. "Good evening. I hope we're not interrupting?"

Hackles up, Bob growled and sniffed at the man's legs. Alex was huge and it wasn't until he was inside that they could see another man equal in size behind him.

"Not at all, come in." Ruby smiled warmly. "Hello, you must be Viktor Petrov?"

"Yes. I am pleased to meet you. Alex speaks of you every day. Many times."

Alex elbowed his friend, but Viktor simply shook Ruby's hand, and they crossed the room to where Scarlett and Violet stood to welcome them both.

"We've eaten, but we're about to have dessert." Violet told them.

"Oh. Are we too early?" Alex consulted his watch.

"No, you're fine." Ruby insisted. "Violet was late home, and we were chatting about the mayor and lost track of time. I can't wait to see the changes. Is the table okay?"

Clearly Ruby had forgotten to tell them about the visitors. Or had she? The sweetest person, Violet could admit that Ruby was adept at getting her own way with the least fuss possible and had a penchant for waifs and strays. Alex had once fit into this category, but no longer. Now that he was recognized as the son of an influential member of the wider community, his status was instantly elevated. Plus, he was about to become a business owner by purchasing the recently burned down and now rebuilt diner, and that was good for Cozy Hollow.

The sisters simply liked him for the man he was. Especially Ruby. Which was probably why Bob settled himself between Alex's chair and Ruby's. George jumped onto the back of the only easy chair in the room and stared at the men who gazed at the fruit crumble Violet placed on the table. Viktor licked his lips.

"Have you eaten?" Scarlett asked with concern. "We have leftovers if you want supper first."

"Yes, thank you ma'am. We already ate." Viktor spoke with an accent just like Alex. "Alex is trying all his recipes out on me to see if they are good enough for his diner. They are better than good." He gave the dessert another longing glance. "But we didn't have dessert."

Scarlett pulled out another chair. "Then take a seat and help yourself. There's plenty."

Ruby collected bowls and spoons and soon the room was filled with sounds of appreciation—coming mostly from the men. Under the table, Bob dropped his head into Violet's lap and she slipped him a morsel of crunchy topping.

"This is delicious." Alex ran a finger around his bowl. "Can I have the recipe for the diner, Scarlett?"

"I don't see why not. I may have a couple of others that you can use too."

Viktor pointed at his almost empty bowl. "Is that a good thing to share recipes if you both make and sell food?"

"We have a café, and though we sell cakes and pies, we don't sell desserts as such," Violet explained. "Plus, it's good to help other businesses."

He looked dubious and Ruby filled them in on why it was hard for him to appreciate. "Viktor was working at the factory that Alex's father owns, and he's only ever known the corporation's cut throat way of doing things. He quit when Alex left and is going to work in the diner."

"He is a hard worker," Alex said proudly, and Viktor ducked his head in embarrassment.

"Are you a chef?" Scarlett enquired.

He tilted his hand back and forth and swallowed another mouthful. "Not so much. Only what Alex has shown me. I am learning every day."

Alex nodded. "In Russia we have different food. Now I must learn to cook what the people from here prefer."

"Well, I'd like to try your traditional food sometime. It could be a huge draw card for the tourists."

Alex smiled at Ruby. "I thought we would make some for the grand opening. That way we will know if they have a place."

"Great idea." Violet loved trying different food. "Let us know if you need a hand with anything."

"Thank you. Ruby also offered." His cheeks pinked when he gazed at her once more.

"Good luck with finding staff," Violet said sincerely.

Alex raised an eyebrow. "You don't have a replacement yet at the café for the woman who left?"

"No. Aunt Olivia is helping when she can, but she'll be doing the handover of her craft store as well. I'd suggest you get onto it right away."

He nodded. "Perhaps you can help me write something for the paper?"

Violet shook her head. "I'm sure Ruby would be better at that than me. She's the wordsmith."

"I would like that," Alex said softly.

This time Viktor elbowed him.

CHAPTER FOUR

It was the weekend and Violet drove to Destiny. Unlike Portland, it wasn't a large city, but it was a large town, making it the next best thing with plenty of second-hand dealers and shops dotted around the well-laid out streets.

Phin rented a place just off Main Street, and she found a parking space a few doors down. She pressed the buzzer for his apartment noticing that the building was very old, and this fitted perfectly with her mood.

He waited in the hall and gave her a gentle hug. "It's wonderful to see you again, Violet."

Oddly she was a little sorry when he let go and the reaction startled her. She was not a needy person, so again it had to come down to guilt at leaving Scarlett to cope without her and needing more reassurance she was doing the right thing. "You too. Are you working on anything interesting right now?"

He chuckled. "Someone sounds eager to get started. I have several items which I've kept to one side to show you, but wouldn't you like a hot drink first?"

She shook her head. "I had to stop for gas and bought a coffee there."

"In that case, come into the sitting room, which is also my office while I'm here." He pulled out a seat at the antique desk. "How are you?"

"Great. I'm looking forward to starting my training next month and I've been studying hard."

"That's good to hear. I wondered when you decided to stay at the café whether you would change your mind about being an assessor."

She gasped at the idea. "No way! It's what's kept me going."

He laughed. "Oh dear. Is it that bad?"

"Worse. No, I'm exaggerating. But you know baking is not what I want to do."

He nodded. "Sometimes you have to wait for things to work out, but here you are and having you here makes an old man happy."

"Hah! You're not old."

"Good response. I have lunch prepared which won't compare with your food, but there's a diner on the corner for our other meals." He had a pained expression. "I took the liberty of checking out your accommodation. I hope it will be satisfactory. "

She laughed, having driven past the place before coming here. "I know it's not much, but it was the right price and fine for one night. Plus, it has free parking and is close by."

"If you're sure?" He shrugged apologetically. "Even if it was appropriate to have you stay here, there's no spare bedroom."

"Please don't worry, and I meant to say that this is a lovely building."

"My uncle owns it," he said proudly. "which is why I was

lucky enough to rent the apartment on short notice. Now, where should we begin?"

"If you don't mind, I have something for you to look at. It's supposed to be an heirloom."

He took a seat. "By the look on your face, I see there is some doubt."

She pulled the ring from her pocket, unwrapped it gently and laid it on the baize of the jewelry plate sitting in the middle of the desk. "That's right and the owner is desperate to know if it's authentic. His ring was made at the end of the first world war for an elite squad that fought in Germany who survived numerous raids."

Phin's eyes twinkled and he picked up the ring, turning it over and over, his thumb rubbing every surface, before he pulled a loupe from his top pocket. This round instrument was used by jewelers and watchmakers to see things in minute detail such as carat and clarity in diamonds, but also as a magnifier. "Let us see what is revealed."

Again, he turned the ring over, but this time in slow motion as he studied it using the eye piece. "This is well made…and a replica."

"I knew it!" Violet had witnessed Phin make a call like this many times before. Although, it was never as thrilling as when it was something close to you. When he'd authenticated a book which changed the Finch girls lives financially, she thought her heart would burst. True, this item wasn't theirs, but now that Arthur was a friend she felt nearly as invested in the outcome. Or maybe that's how she would always feel with a discovery because following the history was just as fascinating as how you got there.

Phin smiled knowingly as if he could read her thoughts. "A star pupil already."

"I wish. My client noticed that a bump in the metal was now smooth, which made me think it wasn't as sturdy as it should be if it was authentic," she admitted. "And as far as he knew it was never out of his possession."

"How interesting." He raised an eyebrow. "I suspect there is more to this story."

"So much more." Violet explained what had happened and he grew excited.

"There are more items missing from this era?"

"Many and from earlier. It makes me wonder if some of the ones he has hidden away are also replacements. I wish I'd had time to check more of them—and that I'd already done my training."

"Soon enough." He chuckled, then squared the tray while he pondered something.

She waited patiently and was rewarded.

"I am intrigued by the fact there could be so many items that need authenticating. Perhaps I could look at them if your friend wouldn't mind."

She wasn't sure how Arthur would feel about a stranger touching his things, but he had met Phin before, and she honestly thought he could help him. "It will be hard enough to tell him they could all be fakes, and I don't think he'd let any more out of his sight."

Phin considered this in his usual way with a finger tapping his chin. "What if I came back to Cozy Hollow when you return?"

"You'd do that?" she gasped as such an unexpected offer.

"I will if you think your 'client'," he winked, "will allow me into his home."

"Actually, you've already met him. It's the Mayor."

His eyes widened. Phin had seen mean Arthur in action and had yet to witness the transformation. "Goodness. He was an angry man before, so this must have tipped him over the edge."

"He's changed a great deal since then." She saw his disbelief and had to explain. "Arthur had a deep-seated grudge with my family which was made worse by PTSD and the wrong medication. After his treatment, he willingly brought out into the open his past feelings and actions, inspecting them just like an antique, and owned up to his flaws and misdeeds. The acknowledgement and good things he's done since repaired a lot of the damage he did, which makes us all a good deal happier."

"I dare say." Phin sounded dubious. "If he's not hounding you to leave town any more, then life would indeed be much better."

It was sweet that Phin cared about the Finch family and with a grateful heart she was ready to throw herself into the training schedule she was required to do in order to gain an assessor's certificate. It wasn't going to happen anytime soon, but she was powering ahead with the online course that Phin had produced as well as studying art at night school to finish the degree she halted to help care for their mother.

Phin ran his finger down the first page of the curriculum. "A great deal of this you know, and now it's a matter of doing the practical alongside the theoretical, which will speed up the process. Although I work mainly with books, I have several other items for you to check over this weekend and we'll include looking up the details of the piece of the mayor's collection as part of your practice. I know you're anxious to begin work and anything you do that is documented as your hours of training will shorten the time to qualify. "

"I am, but I want to be sure I know enough." She couldn't help grinning. "I never thought that helping Arthur might be included this way and it sounds perfect."

Phin waggled the same finger. "I'll remind you that my name will appear on your paperwork, so don't imagine I'm doing you any favors, or that I would let you out into the world as a bona fide assessor without being sure you were up to it."

"I understand completely." His confidence in her meant a great deal and she'd do her utmost to be good at it—while she aimed for great.

The first item Phin pulled out from a chunky safe was a letter opener. Unwrapped from its velvet cover, the handle looked silver and so did the blade. It was tainted with age and missing jewels in several places.

"This is for you to keep." Phin opened his other hand and showed her another loupe. "A gift from teacher to student so you begin in the right way."

It wasn't new; the place to hold it was smooth from use. "I love it! Thank you." A lump in her throat stopped her from saying more, but his eyes twinkled again as if he understood.

The first thing she did was to sniff the knife—silver had no smell at all. Then she held it to the light to see if it sparkled the way silver should. Next she checked to see if the surface was peeling which would indicate a layer of paint rather than silver.

Finally, she brought the knife as close to the loupe as possible without the item becoming blurry and slowly studied every inch just as he'd taught her. What she was looking for was any markings to indicate the date of manufacture and other information about the knife. There would hopefully be the mark of the manufacturer or silversmith and a silver hallmark to indicate the purity, if it was in fact made of silver. She took her time, aware of Phin watching, but not disturbed by it.

Eventually she looked up and tried not to smile at her certainty. "I believe this contains .925 silver from the late 1800's."

"Why do you say that?"

"Below the number 25, which means .925 in the game, is the symbol of the maker as well as the year.

"Excellent. What about this?" He swapped the letter opener for a gold necklace.

It took next to no time before she saw the tell-tale signs. "This is a fake." She tapped an area near the clasp. "Underneath the gold is bronze, and it's had a very bad patch-up right here."

"Perfect. And what about this?" He pointed to a small wooden stool.

Violet knew right away what it was, but opened the folded cloth that Phin pointed to and placed it over part of the desk. Next she lifted the stool gently and set it down on the cloth, taking her time looking it over, determined not to rush and miss something. It was easy to guess or think you knew, but until you checked every detail the eye could fool you into believing what you wanted to see.

"This is an early to mid 1900's foot stool. It would be approximately 80 years old. The top is hand embroidered but is much newer. Probably still late 1900's."

He clapped his hands and bowed. "Well done. I'm very proud of how far you've come in a short space of time. I can see your extra study is paying dividends."

She blushed at his praise. He'd been very firm with her when she first began to train and pushed her every step of the way. His words lifted her spirits in ways she couldn't describe. Having found her path, nothing would stop her now. She grimaced. There was just the small matter of getting someone to take her place in the café.

Aunt Olivia was doing well, but she couldn't do the hours to cover Violet when she left next month unless the craft store sold. Pushing that along was one more thing to add to her to-do list, and every bit as important as studying.

Phin packed up the smaller pieces and replaced them in

his safe. "When you return home look at every piece and write a report on them for me to check when I come."

"When will that be?"

He pulled a leather diary toward him and flipped through a few pages. "I could make it next weekend?"

"That would be awesome." It would be great to have him around to check her work, but also to look at anything of Arthur's that might be fake. Hopefully he would have better news for the mayor.

Violet was buzzing from the affirmation that she did have a talent and it was for something she truly enjoyed. Plus, she had another whole day tomorrow to do more assessing with her mentor. Meeting him was the luckiest day of her life and having Phin come to Cozy Hollow was frosting on the cake.

CHAPTER FIVE

As soon as Violet got home on Sunday night, Bob ran to the door and barreled into her. They all wondered when this delight at seeing them might settle down to something less physical. He was a rescue dog, devoted to them, and very needy, so maybe never.

Ruby grinned at Violet's attempt to remain upright. "He's been waiting for you. I guess he heard the car."

"Get down Bob." Violet put a finger in the air, and he sat, his tail thumping the floor. She gave the loving Labrador the scratch and attention he craved. "Where's George?" The tabby who also loved them, was far more aloof, but exceptionally nosey and it was strange he didn't come to greet her as well.

Ruby chewed her bottom lip. "He's keeping Scarlett company in the sitting room."

"Oh-oh. What happened now?"

"Arthur's in the hospital."

Violet gasped and dropped her hold-all with a clatter making Bob run for cover under the table. "What? He was fine on Friday. Was it a heart attack?"

Ruby's baby blue eyes welled. "No. He was run off the road, yesterday."

"Is he okay? Why didn't you phone me?"

"You were training, and we decided that you wouldn't want an interruption that wasn't an emergency. I promise, there was nothing you could have done if you came home early. I had no idea you'd be so upset, otherwise I would have." She wiped her eyes with the heel of her hands. "Scarlett says he's doing okay, Vi."

She didn't know what to say so she went to the sitting room, where Scarlett and George were snuggled under a blanket. The tabby's head peered over the edge of the blanket from where he was perched on Scarlett's chest.

Any anger she felt about her sisters not letting her know that Arthur was hurt slipped away. "Arthur can't be that good, if you're so sad."

Scarlett gave her a watery smile. "He's doing fine. I just feel so bad for him. You should have seen him in the hospital bed—so confused and upset that he was being targeted."

"I could have gone to see him before I came home," Violet said, then stilled as her sister's words sunk in. "He thinks this was on purpose?"

"After everything that's happened, don't you?" Ruby gulped and commenced hiccupping.

Violet put her arm around her shoulder. "It does seem that someone wants him out of the picture. Now I don't know what to do. Arthur wants me to go through his collection and check the authenticity of each item and Phin said he would come next weekend to look over everything. He said it can be included in my training and I was really looking forward to the experience and knowing if I was right."

Ruby stared at her in horror. "Oh, Violet. Don't you care about him at all?"

Violet grimaced. "Of course, I do, Rubes. Didn't I ask if he was okay?"

Ruby sighed. "I guess."

Now Violet was truly offended. "You know I don't hold any grudge over his treatment of us and I respect him for trying to make amends. He brought me into his problem by asking for my help, and though I won't pretend I'm not intrigued by the items being stolen or swapped—can't it be about both things?"

She hadn't intended for her voice to raise the way it had and bit her lip against the shock on their faces. Always the snippiest of the three of them, with the middle child syndrome waiting to be unleashed at any provocation—until recently—the change in her wasn't total, but couldn't they see how hard she tried to be more even tempered? "Sorry, she muttered."

Ruby immediately backtracked. "No, I'm sorry. I know it's taken you a bit longer than Scarlett and me to get used to having Arthur in our lives, but you're right about the fact he called you. Plus, it says a lot about how highly he regards your talents."

"It's true, Vi." Scarlett smiled. "We're all finding our way and sometimes we forget how it used to be not so long ago. Ruby and I are so glad you've found this passion and if helping Arthur is mutually beneficial then we couldn't be happier."

Violet took them at their word, but now she wasn't sure if she should pursue it. "You don't think it's inappropriate?"

"The timing could be better," Scarlett admitted. "But it may be the best way of finding out who is trying to hurt Arthur. The only one who may have a real problem with it is the sheriff."

"That's okay, though." Ruby grinned mischievously. "Scarlett can take care of him for you."

While it was obvious by the raised eyebrow that Scarlett didn't totally approve of the joke, they all laughed.

Still chuckling, Ruby curled up in a chair. "Tell us all about your time with Phin. You looked so happy when you got home, and I feel bad that we've destroyed that for you."

Violet shook her head. "I will once you tell me about Arthur. You said he got run off the road?"

"That's right. He told me he got a call to check out a huge pothole that had suddenly appeared and the caller wanted something done as soon as possible because it damaged his car."

"Who was it that made the call?"

Scarlett shrugged. "He doesn't think they mentioned a name, just rattled off directions and slammed down the phone."

"Well, that is suspicious. Then what happened?"

"He was driving down the road that runs parallel with the main road to Destiny when a car pulled out from a driveway and smashed into him. Arthur's car spun 360 and landed in a ditch. He was knocked out for a short time and the paramedics took him straight to Destiny with a suspected concussion from his head hitting the windscreen."

"Anything else? No broken bones?"

"Fortunately, there's only some bruising." Scarlett tucked her legs under her and patted the sofa beside her, but before Violet could sit, Bob was up on it leaving a much smaller space for Violet to squeeze into.

Scarlett snorted and scratched the Labrador's head. "Lucky we like you, Bob, because you are very annoying." Looking at her adoringly, Bob slapped a big paw on her knee. "When I saw him earlier today he was naturally upset that someone tried to hurt him, and also desperately worried about his house being unoccupied. I offered to house sit and sleep over, but he wasn't keen on the idea. He said it wasn't safe."

"After this, I'm inclined to believe him. Does Arthur or Nate know who hit his car?"

"Arthur saw a black sedan fly by as he slid off the road, and so far Nate doesn't have a clue."

Violet had a bad feeling that she recognized. "You know if this person is connected to the stealing, that means they hit Arthur deliberately to get him out of the way. With an unoccupied house, they'd have total access to his possessions. That feels like we're playing into the thief's hands."

Deep in thought, they all jumped when Bob barked. He ran to the front door nearby heralding the knock that came after. Bob looked alert, but not concerned. It was unusual to have someone use this entrance, because the drive lead down the side of the house, so everyone used the back door, including most visitors. Being the closest, Violet opened the door to find the sheriff in uniform, clasping his hat in front of him.

"Hi, Violet. Can I come in for a few minutes?"

"Sure, we're in the sitting room."

"I saw the light through the curtains and guessed as much." He removed his hat and followed her inside, heading straight for Scarlett with a warmer smile. "Hi, Scarlett. Ruby."

The latter got a cursory nod and Violet winked at Ruby before she perched on the arm of her sister's chair. "Your ears must be burning, Sheriff."

He barely glanced at her. "Why's that."

"We've been discussing this business with Arthur and his treasures. He was worried before and, after this accident, I think he has every right to be, don't you?"

Nate sat beside Scarlett, which didn't impress Bob who was too late to claim his space and sat in front of the sheriff giving him the death stare. George clambered up the arm to sit beside him and likewise stared.

Nate shook his head, well used to these two and their over-protective antics. "Slow down a bit, Violet. There's no evidence that the two things are related."

"Then why are you here?" She asked in what she thought was a reasonable manner, but Scarlett's frown indicated maybe it wasn't.

"I wanted Scarlett, and all of you, to know that I have my new deputy checking on Arthur's place overnight."

"Thank goodness. I'd hate anything else to be stolen."

He made a rude noise in the back of his throat. "Like I said, Violet, we don't know if there has been a theft."

She crossed her arms. "Arthur said you didn't believe him, but it's true and I can prove it."

"Is that so?"

She pulled the ring out of her pocket. "This is Arthur's, but it's a forgery and before you remind me that I'm not qualified to say that with anything more than my opinion, Phin agreed with my assessment. Which means, since Arthur has so many other things that he's not sure about, I need to check the house."

He pursed his lips. "Even if that's true, you'll have to wait until Arthur's back on his feet. I can't let you wander around his house without his consent, and I just heard that the doctor wants to keep him in at least another night if he hasn't improved by tomorrow."

"But he was doing fine when I saw him this morning," Scarlett exclaimed.

"I know, but his eye sight is still blurry and it's not coming right as fast as they hoped. It's just a precaution, so no need to panic."

"Poor Arthur," Ruby said sadly, and Bob hurried to her side to nuzzle her hands.

Violet nodded. "This is not good news on any level."

"I've seen that look before. I don't want any of you near his place until he's back home," Nate warned.

"Not even a quick peek at the property in daylight?" Violet asked after a small silence which earned her a narrowed-eyed look from her eldest sister.

"What do you mean by that?" Nate asked.

"You may have the house being watched tonight but I can't imagine you have the resources to do that around the clock. We could also take turns checking tomorrow until Arthur gets home, so there's no opportunity for a would-be thief."

Scarlett coughed to draw their attention. "Violet means we would do a circuit around the property and leave once we're sure no one is there. In our car."

"That's it?" He snorted. "No poking around or exploring the grounds?"

"Exactly."

"Only, I've never known the three of you to stick to the plan."

"That's a little unfair," Scarlett protested.

"Is it really?"

"So, that's a no?" Violet pressed.

There was a long pause, before he answered. "It should be, but I see no harm in you driving by. As long as that's all you do. No getting out to check on anything, and you phone me if you see anything out of the ordinary."

"Absolutely, thanks, Nate," she gushed.

"Don't make me regret it," he growled.

"We wouldn't dream of it. Coffee?"

"I'd love some, but I better get going." Nate stood, and looking at Scarlett, who got to her feet, he hesitated.

"Are you heading to Arthur's?" Violet asked, trying not to smirk at their awkwardness.

"I am, and no, you can't come."

Ruby nudged her in the side, and she didn't say anything until Scarlett and Nate were outside. "I wonder what they're talking about?"

"Shhh. I'm trying to hear."

"It's about time they started dating properly."

"Mmmm."

The door closed and Scarlett came back into the room decidedly pink-cheeked.

"Thanks for pushing the check-in on Arthur's place."

"You didn't leave me much choice, Vi. I suspected you weren't going to leave the idea alone and it's better if we keep on the sheriff's right side."

"Speaking of that, did he ask you out?" Ruby asked casually.

The color deepened and Scarlett picked up George, using him as a shield. "We're going to the movies Friday night."

"Wow." Violet tutted. "Could he be any more romantic."

Scarlett waved away the sarcasm. "It's enough right now. I'm busy at the café and he has a lot of cases, including the business with Arthur."

"At least it's a step in the right direction," Ruby exclaimed delightedly.

"Someone's living vicariously," Violet teased. "What about Alex. How's that going?"

Their youngest sister's eyes danced. "Alex and I are good friends, and you know I'm helping him with some ideas around the setup for his new diner."

"Wouldn't Scarlett be better at that? She knows baking and cafés inside and out." While this was the truth, the reasoning behind Ruby wanting to help was as clear as a pastry glaze and Violet wasn't above teasing either of her sisters when she got the chance. Small pleasures and all that.

"Like she told you, Scarlett's busy," Ruby reminded her.

"It's easier for him to drop by the library." Scarlett defended Ruby, but they all knew she was simply happy to deflect the conversation from the budding relationship with Nate.

It seemed that it was only Violet who was missing a love interest—which suited her fine. Bob and George were the men in her life and that was enough for any career woman.

CHAPTER SIX

Violet was up early and more unusual than that, up before Scarlett, who was still curled up in her bed with Bob across the bottom of it, regardless that he had a bed in the corner of the room.

She tiptoed around the place getting ready and making coffee. While she was putting out food for Bob and George, the big tabby made an appearance. He gave her his customary rub against the leg and hoovered up his food before sniffing Bob's. Without so much as a cursory lick, deeming it inferior to his own food, George flicked his tail and headed out through the cat flap on the back door.

She was just about to leave when Scarlett appeared still in her pajamas, Bob trailing behind her. "What's wrong?"

The pointed reference that Violet was not an early riser by choice was fair. "Nothing. I just want to drive by Arthur's before I head to the café."

Scarlett crossed her arms. "You do realise it's still dark outside."

"Not for too much longer."

"Nate said not to go there in the dark."

"Well, I thought I'd drive around a bit and check out the lanes around it. I have my phone and I'll lock the car doors."

Scarlett narrowed her eyes. "Since I'm awake now, you better come and get me after that, so Ruby can have the other car."

Ruby often helped in the café for an hour or two in the morning before heading to the library, but not on Mondays, which was their slowest day, and Violet had forgotten. "Okay, and I won't be too long."

"You better not be. And take Bob."

"Bob? You're not serious."

The dog in question bounded into the room, his tongue lolling happily.

Scarlett tapped her slippered foot. "He's a good watchdog."

"Sure, if licking to death was a weapon."

"Just take him, will you?"

They stared at each other for a moment, more words not necessary. Violet nodded, and before leaving gave Bob time to wolf down his breakfast. She wasn't about to do something crazy, and Scarlett would have to trust her, but if taking Bob along made her sister feel better, then Violet had no problem with that. They both liked to get to the bottom of things and had a dislike of the unknown. Especially when it concerned people they cared about.

After driving around the lanes near Arthur's, it was still dark as she headed up the driveway and came to a stop at the side of the house. Nate wouldn't be happy about it, but once they got to the café, they had to make bread and all the other goodies to fill the shelves. There wouldn't be a chance to check on Arthur's again until late morning and she hadn't seen anything of the new deputy.

Turning off the lights and engine, the trees created shadows to her right. As her eyesight adjusted, the closest branches suddenly looked like fingers clawing at the windows. Violet shuddered and forced herself to look at the rest of the place. Nothing moved, except the slight undulation of trees. The silence was oppressive, possibly due to an active imagination. Bob slithered over from the back seat to the passenger seat and flopped down beside her, watching her every move.

"We're on lookout for burglars. Do you see any?"

His head tilted to the side, before he peered out the front and side windows. Then he looked back, sighed, and lay down.

"I didn't think so," she chuckled. "Everything looks fine to me as well."

She waited ten minutes and was about to leave when a light came from the second floor of the house. Her heart hammered.

A torch light!

Violet considered the way it moved in an up and down arc, and, as it didn't flicker, this confirmed her assumption it could only be a torch, or possibly a large candle. The light moved from one window to another, then disappeared.

Pulling out her phone she called Nate who didn't pick up. It was early, so she left a frantic message then called the station. Bob stood, his tail wagging. The station wasn't too far away and very soon deputy Glasson came running across the lawn. Small towns didn't have many deputies available for patrols and watching Arthur's place couldn't be done the whole night, so he must have come from the station.

She opened her door and he leaned on it, breathing heavy, his gaze searching the house.

"Thanks for the tip-off, but what are you doing here, Violet?"

She quickly explained her conversation with the sheriff and pointed to where she'd last seen the light. "They may still be inside, but over the other side of the hall in the upstairs bedrooms, which would explain why we can't see the light now."

He considered his option before making a decision. "Okay. Get back in the car, and I'll check it out. Lock the door."

He said it firmly, but she detected a small shake of his hand when he pushed his hat securely on his head. Though she wanted to go with him, that simple act scared her enough to do as he said. Plus, there was no denying Nate would be furious that she was still here. Not to mention her sisters.

She was so intent on trying to see where deputy Glasson was, or if the light had moved elsewhere, Bob's growl, followed soon after by a knock on the window beside her face made her shriek. "Nate!"

Unlocking the door, she jumped out almost knocking him over followed by Bob who insisted on Nate patting him. "Did you get him?"

"Get who?" he growled.

She no longer had to wonder how annoyed he would be. "Didn't you receive my message?"

"No. I was off duty for a couple of hours and coming to check on the house as promised on my way to the office. Remember promises? You said you wouldn't come here in the dark."

"Yes, yes," she waved his annoyance away, not sure how else to stem his justified tirade. "Deputy Glasson is checking on a light I saw moving around inside the house on the upstairs floor."

"What?" His hand reached for the gun on his hip, and he swung around to survey the house in a fluid movement.

She was impressed by his change into Sheriff mode and felt safer having him here. "I was sitting in the dark about to leave for the bakery 'as promised' when I saw the light."

His eyes didn't stop scanning. "Are you sure?"

"Absolutely. I can't say for certain if it was a torch or a candle, but it was definitely there. Aren't you going to check?"

With an impatient gesture he pulled out a small torch and pushed her back toward the car. "Inside, now," he growled. "And lock the doors."

She sighed, but ushered Bob back in the car first, much to his objection as he tugged at her hold of his collar, and soon Nate was out of sight. She hoped she hadn't sent two good men into danger. Sure, they dealt with that often enough, but this seemed sinister and that thought caused her to scan the area near the house again, not forgetting behind her in case someone snuck up on the car. Her mind played tricks, thinking she saw things amongst the shadows, and the moments until she saw them walking toward her it were some of the longest of her life.

They seemed okay, and their guns were holstered, so she got out again, making sure Bob stayed inside this time, which he wasn't pleased about, and whined at the door. "Did you find anyone?" It was a silly question, since they were clearly alone, but she was filled with relief they were safe.

"It looks like they got away." Nate sounded even more annoyed than he had before as he shone his torch around once more. "I'd like to get inside but we don't have the key and breaking in seems extreme when there's no danger to anyone."

Violet was mentally agreeing, when she had an epiphany and slapped her forehead then reached into the glove compartment. She handed him a large front door key. "Arthur gave Ruby this spare ages ago so she could access his library whenever she had time. I'm so sorry that I forgot about it. Ruby couldn't bring herself to use it, so it's been in the car for months and none of us gave it a second thought all that time."

Even in the dark, she sensed his frustration with her rambling before he snatched from her hand.

"I know, back in the car, right?" She scrambled in without waiting for an answer.

Inside the house, but not switching on any lights, the men moved through each room aided by their torches. Violet ran her fingers impatiently around the steering wheel, silently urging them on.

Suddenly, a figure darted from the back of the house and through the hedge on her right. It happened so fast she had to consider for a second if she'd imagined it.

Without another thought, she jumped out of the car and yelled for Nate as loud as she could. He came running like a hare and she pointed to the space the person had disappeared through. "Someone came running out the back. They went that way!"

With barely a missed beat he ran after them followed by the deputy—and Bob! She called him several times, but he didn't come back, which left Violet on her own. Of course, the thief could have an accomplice, and now that she'd alerted the whole town that she was here, she should probably get back in the car, but after a couple of minutes when no one else appeared, she turned on the car lights and made her way down the side of the house stopping at a small gap in the bushes. Broken branches on both sides showed where the three of them had busted through.

She pulled out her phone and shone the torch app around her. There on a branch she saw a few strands of something. They were thicker than a cobweb and darker in color. Hair! She was pretty sure of it.

Muted voices came from beyond the hedge, and she moved back a few paces before the men returned. Bob squeezed through another gap, twigs and leaves decorating his fur. He pranced around like he'd had fun. She grabbed his collar and brought him to heel.

"Careful, Nate," she said softly. "It looks like some hair is stuck on the branch just in front of you."

It went quiet and then a hand came out to push the branch away and Nate stepped into the light. He glared at her before pulling out a glove and wrapping it around the strands. When both men were clear he opened his hand and took a closer look at the find.

"Looks a bit light to be yours or deputy Glasson's hair," she noted with interest.

"Do you ever listen?" he growled.

"I try, but what should I have done when I saw him come flying across the grass?"

"How about beeping the horn?"

Violet gaped. "Oh. I guess I could have done that if I had thought of it."

He made a disgusted sound in the back of his throat and placed the strands in a Ziploc bag, then tucked it into his jacket.

She had to ask. "Did you see who it was?"

He ran his fingers through his hair before replacing his hat. "No, they were too far in front of us and had a getaway car in the next road which screamed off before we could get to it."

"Was it a dark sedan like the one that ran Arthur off the road?"

"Violet, go home or get to the café. I don't care which."

There was no mistaking the 'or else' inflection. "Thanks for reminding me. I have to pick up Scarlett and get to the café right away. I said I wouldn't be long, so she's going to be worried and probably not too happy when I tell her what happened."

He sighed heavily. "Will she really be surprised by another of your exploits?"

"Maybe not, but she'll be furious if we're late opening." Knowing that he was just as furious, she slipped back into the car with Bob and with a wave headed home.

Scarlett was pacing on the driveway, bag in hand and a face like thunder. She yanked open the door, got in with a thump and slammed it. Violet flinched. Luckily they didn't have close neighbors.

"Don't be mad until you hear what happened."

With a groan, her sister leaned her head back. "It's too late, or too early for explanations. I haven't made up my mind, but we're late so let Bob out then just drive and allow me to fume a little while I try to be happy that you're safe."

CHAPTER SEVEN

On the opposite side of the counter, a lump of bread dough was getting a workout, and Violet wasn't sure if Scarlett's batch would be edible by the time she was done.

Violet had finished the story some time ago, but her sister wasn't warming to the idea that she'd helped in any way. "I swear, I didn't do it intentionally. I saw the light and had to call someone. Then the guy was simply there in front of me, and I had to..."

"You didn't have to be there all this time, and what you *had* to do was call and let me know you were safe and not lying in a ditch somewhere—or worse."

"Okay. Next time..."

Scarlett punched the dough once more. "Do you hear yourself? There is to be no next time!"

Violet stiffened. "While I appreciate I scared you, I think this might be the time you reflect on the things you've done that felt right at the time, yet weren't exactly what the sheriff, or me and Ruby were comfortable with. You were keen enough to find the answers to various mysteries you've been involved in, so why can't you give me a little credit for helping today?"

"Those were different circumstances."

"Tell me how."

Scarlett's mouth opened and closed a couple of times. "I'm the eldest and sometimes I have to make tough decisions."

"By a couple of years, and we are all adults now and capable of making our own decisions, so that excuse is irrelevant. If this were you instead of me involved in a crime, you'd be in boots and all trying to figure out who did it, which is all I'm doing and, in case you hadn't noticed, I wasn't hurt."

Scarlett dropped dough into pans not as carefully as usual, which spoke of how upset she was. "But I didn't know that, and it's my job to keep you safe," she said through gritted teeth.

Violet sighed. "I know you think that and I'm touched that you care so much, but you have to let go. I'm a big girl. We all are, and we can take care of ourselves."

The door opened and Olivia came inside with a rush. "It's so cold out. Did you see that Arthur's place is surrounded by deputies?"

Their aunt was their mother's sister and, though she had a craft store to run, helped out in the bakery most mornings. She was very attuned to their moods and stopped talking with her coat half off. "Please do not tell me that you girls are involved in whatever is happening at Arthur's."

"I'm not," Scarlett said emphatically, and placed her bread dough in the warmer drawer to rise.

Olivia raised an eyebrow as she dropped her coat on the peg by the door. "I guess that leaves you, Violet?"

Shoulders hunched; she should have anticipated this. Now Violet had to repeat everything, and would need to do so again when Ruby heard about it. Then there was Olivia's craft group. Those whose ears and tongues would be working overtime once they knew Violet had first-hand knowledge about the situation occurring up the street.

Still, there was no way around it. Olivia wouldn't be deterred, so Violet moved on to making muffins while she told the story as she knew it.

"Let me get this straight," Olivia had chocolate cakes on the go and was stalling putting on the mixer so she could hear. "Someone is stealing things from Arthur Tully, and they may have tried to kill him?"

Violet nodded. "That's still conjecture, but yes."

"Well, he's made plenty of enemies in his past," Olivia tutted. "But murder does seem a bit of a stretch in Cozy Hollow."

Scarlett raised an eyebrow. "Ah, I think you'll find over the last year or so we have had a couple."

"True but hurting Arthur after he's mended his ways and consequently a few fences since he persecuted you girls seems all kinds of wrong."

"I'm guessing not all the fences," Violet reminded her. As a committee member and the mayor, he had made decisions that had mainly benefited himself, and people around here tended to have long memories.

Olivia sighed. "You may be right."

"What I'm struggling with is, if killing Arthur is what the thief ultimately wants, why all this cat and mouse with the stolen goods. Some were returned and some replaced." Violet was primarily talking to herself as she tried to work through the clues, but Scarlett had a knack for putting two and two together and her sister didn't disappoint.

"It seems to me that they want something specific. What if the other items are merely a ruse to put us off the track of who the thief might be?"

Violet nodded. "That makes sense, only why return them at all?"

"Because it allowed whoever it is to keep looking for the thing or things they really want before the sheriff got involved and started watching the place."

"So now that he is involved, things have changed, right?" Violet chewed her lip for a moment. "With the pressure on, they had to get rid of Arthur, so they could make one last effort."

Patiently frosting cupcakes, Scarlett gave Violet a measured look. "Only, you thwarted them."

Olivia gasped. "Which means you could be in danger too, Violet."

"I was in the car, and I don't think they saw me," Violet said with more positivity than she felt.

"I hope not." Olivia tutted. "This family has been through quite enough and I don't think my heart could take any more drama."

Olivia was still young at 57 and had plenty of stamina, but wasn't above playing the age card to get their sympathy and make them behave the way she thought they ought.

"I appreciate that, but if we can we should help Arthur," Scarlett said in an about face. "He's been so kind to us."

"Hmmm." Olivia digested this for a moment. "While I want to give him the benefit of the doubt, can a leopard change his spots entirely?"

Scarlett wasn't having that. "Aunt! I know how difficult it is to think differently after the way he treated us, but he's tried so hard to make up for it."

"I just remembered how depressed you girls were when your mom passed away and what a terrible time you had trying to make the café work with him fighting you every step of the way."

"We were all grieving—including Arthur. Only we didn't

know that or why." Violet reminded their aunt, who had kept the secret of his infatuation with their mom for too long. It had turned out to be a huge mistake which she usually owned.

This time Olivia's face reddened. "All that business with him trying to run you out of town stuck in my craw and I admit I'm taking longer than most to forget it."

"No one said anything about forgetting. He was part of mom's life and she loved him as a friend. While she would have been horrified if she'd seen him behave the way he did, sickness or not, he never would have done so, if she'd been alive."

"You're right, and Lilac would have talked him around, found out what was wrong with him and promptly forgiven him." Olivia sniffed.

Scarlett nodded. "I'm sure Mom does."

Now they were all sniffing.

"Lucky Ruby's not here, otherwise we'd be sobbing messes," Violet noted, and the other two grinned misty-eyed.

"If I don't get the bread in the oven there won't be any to sell."

With that Scarlett got them back on track and after wiping their faces and washing hands, they flew through the necessary baking before opening for the day. The first customers were the usual and potentially too early to notice anything out of the ordinary had taken place. By 9 a.m. that had changed. Not only had the news travelled, but along came the craft group to get any juicy details from whomever might have some.

Olivia poured the four ladies coffee and took orders for the berry muffins Violet had made. The café had a new flavor of cupcake or muffin every day and it was usually the first item to sell out, because most of the regulars wanted to say they'd tried it. To be fair, that came about due to the craft group's competitive nature and how free they were with their comments, and more often than not, loud compliments, which was great for business.

"These look lovely, Violet. I heard you made them today," Gail Norman called across the room

She was at the counter and chuckled to herself. The café wasn't so large that you couldn't hear practically everything said without raising your voice. "That's right. I hope you all enjoy them."

"We always do, and I love strawberry flavor on anything."

Violet smiled genuinely. Once upon a time if their mom or Scarlett hadn't baked it, they were reluctant to try any of Violet's baking, but they were less choosy these days, if not effusive in their praise. Ruby had been brought into the good books early on. Of course, back then Violet was angry at being forced to work in the café when all she wanted to do was look at old things and find out more about them. The two things combined may have had more to do with her treatment than she'd cared to admit until recently.

The café was Scarlett's baby, but it had to be said that with all the dramas they'd gone through together there was a pleasure in working beside her sisters, and now their aunt. The time spent together would be missed when she began her career proper, and she never thought she would feel that way.

The bell over the door chimed and Nate marched in. He did well to hide the grimace that flashed for the briefest moment when he saw the ladies who were already demanding his attention.

"Yoo-hoo, Sheriff. Any news on poor Arthur or his house?"

"Arthur is doing better, and that's all I have to report. Violet, a word if you have time?" he nodded to the kitchen and she obediently led the way, leaving Olivia to serve their muffins.

Scarlett stopped frosting cupcakes and followed them. Intuitively, they walked as far back into the room as possible before he spoke again, keeping his voice low.

"The mayor is coming home this afternoon."

"I thought he had to stay in the hospital a while longer," Violet reminded him.

"He was advised to, but you know Arthur. Since I don't have the manpower to watch his place twenty-four seven, I asked him to hire someone to stay with him, but he refused."

Violet tilted her head. "Are you suggesting I offer?"

"No way," he said firmly. "Only, I don't know of anyone in town who would fit the criteria of being able to handle themselves if they did come across an intruder on short notice, do you?"

The sisters looked at each other questioningly.

Violet eventually nodded. "I wonder if Alex would know anyone." Alex had worked as security guard for the Carver Corporation out at Harmony Beach for years, but now resided in town. Huge and scary looking until you got to know that he had a soft heart, he was also very taken with Ruby. Violet shook her head at where her thoughts were taking her. "I'd suggest him, but he's desperate to get the diner on its feet and wouldn't be able to spare the time, but maybe he knows of someone needing work."

Nate sighed. "He would have been perfect. Anyone would be crazy to take him on. That's a good suggestion though. I'll go find him and see if he can recommend anyone. Thanks."

"Can I get you a coffee to go?" Scarlett asked softly.

"I'd appreciate it. And maybe one of your delicious looking muffins I saw on the counter."

"Are you sure you want one? I made them," Violet teased knowing he'd assumed they were Scarlett's handiwork.

"Well….," he made out he was having second thoughts, but his eye twinkled. "They do look good, so I'll try my luck."

Violet poked out her tongue and he chuckled all the way to the door with his takeout while Scarlett watched with a huge grin and something a little dreamier in her eyes.

They were a perfect couple, and Violet didn't feel at all jealous how things had worked out. She knew from the start that Nate and Scarlett were destined to be together. Scarlett was the only one who wouldn't accept it entirely, because he had dated Violet once. Violet couldn't figure out if this truly bothered Scarlett or if it was an excuse to stall the relationship.

It looked like both her sisters had found men they were interested in, but Violet thought that the way they were dealing with it seemed like an awful waste of time. All this pussyfooting around when all it would take was for one of them to admit to having feelings drove her crazy. Still, it wasn't worth the fallout to mention this again or try to interfere in any way. Not when she'd just convinced Scarlett to come to terms with Violet's independence.

Plus, she was worried about Arthur being in his house alone. Hopefully Alex could help.

CHAPTER EIGHT

A deputy was removing the tape around Arthur's front door and bundling it into a trash bag when Violet came up the path. She'd walked from the café having organized Ruby to come collect her after she closed the library.

The door was open, and Violet was about to knock, when the deputy glanced up and frowned at her.

"Can I help you?"

She'd never met him before and surmised he must be the new deputy. "Hello, I'm Violet Finch and I've come to see the mayor."

He came to stand in front of the door like a sentry. "I'm afraid he can't have visitors."

She was immediately concerned. "Can't? Because he's too ill, or he just doesn't want any?"

The deputy shrugged. "That's all I've been told, so you may as well move along."

He seemed ambivalent that the difference meant a good deal to her, but was determined to keep her out of the house. While he might only be doing his job, it seemed odd that a deputy was vetting visitors this way and she wondered if Arthur knew.

She tried again in a friendly manner. "Could you please tell him that Violet's here? I think he'll want to see me."

"That's not possible..."

Another man came around the side of the house and towered above the deputy. "It's okay, Deputy Pine. I can vouch for her."

"Hi, Viktor." She was ridiculously glad to see the burly friend of Alex's. Somehow he was less intimidating than the deputy.

"I was told not to let anyone inside," he explained pointedly.

Arthur came out of a side room off the hall. "It's okay, Deputy. Violet is welcome anytime."

His lips pursed. "Just doing my job, Sir."

"Of course, you were, but maybe check with me next time. Come on in, Violet."

"You can go," Viktor told the deputy. "I'm here to take care of the mayor now."

"I'll have to run that by the sheriff," the deputy insisted.

Violet heard the exchange from behind her and when she peeked the men had gone.

She waited until she was further down the hall before she said, "Well, someone takes his job very seriously."

Arthur chuckled. "He certainly does. This is his first week, so I guess he's trying to do things by the book."

"Maybe so. Anyway, I'm so glad you have Viktor."

"I wish I'd thought of a bodyguard sooner," he mused. "It would have made life significantly less stressful."

"I agree, but it wouldn't have stopped you being run off the road."

He blanched. "Thanks for reminding me."

"Sorry." Arthur was looking fine until then and she

wished she hadn't mentioned it, but he was already smiling again.

"No, it's the truth." He touched the bandage on his head. "I can't pretend it didn't happen. At least with Viktor here I feel safer, and I hear I have you to thank for the suggestion."

"I just thought Alex would know of someone who could do the job and Viktor seems a really nice guy. Anyway, I didn't mean to disturb you. I know you need your rest, only I wanted to see for myself that you're okay."

"That's so kind of you and to be honest I wouldn't mind a little company." His voice wobbled and he coughed, perhaps to disguise his emotions which were uncharacteristically on display. "Besides, we have things to discuss. How did you get on with my ring?"

It wasn't exactly good news, so she had to temper the grin that threatened to escape when she thought of how she had come to the same conclusion as Phin. "You were right, it is a forgery. We have a theory, but why do you think the thief replaced it?"

"To stop me from calling the police," he said matter-of-factly.

"Snap! That's exactly what I thought. Except for the stuff that wasn't replaced, and I'm thinking that's because those pieces were too big or too hard to replicate. It's the only answer that fits."

"Hmmm. You might have something about the bigger pieces. I had a knight in the entrance way. He was rather special, though I'm not sure he was worth anything. Something that size would be hard to replicate quickly."

Violet chewed her bottom lip thoughtfully. "But it would be far more obvious that it was gone which doesn't fit our scenario."

He snorted and pointed to the space where the knight had stood. Now there was only a patch of darker flooring to indicate something was missing. "It should have been obvious, but I can't pinpoint exactly when it disappeared. Which is ridiculous—I mean a thing that size you'd think I'd notice right away."

She had to agree and was surprised that he found it amusing. Continuing down the hall they by-passed his study and entered the large kitchen which housed a breakfast area. The remodeling to open up the once separated rooms was relatively new, as were the French doors which opened onto a patio area and overlooked the back yard. There was also a path that led back around to the driveway and along the side of the house to the front and the main road. "I love what you've done with this room and how you've captured the gorgeous view."

"It's my favorite place in the house. To be honest, I prefer it over my study. The sun comes in most of the day and even the winter weather doesn't detract from the view." He sighed. "Of course, the weeds are creeping in now that my gardener is gone."

"A few weeds couldn't stop it looking beautiful," Violet said, having noticed that the previously manicured yard wasn't up to the same standard as the front of the house, and now she knew why. It seemed that Arthur had lost both his cleaner/cook and his gardener at the same time. And something else occurred to her. "How do you come into the house when you get home?"

"I use these French doors. Like I said, this is my favorite room in the house, so it makes sense. I..." He blinked furiously. "Wait. I see where you're going with this."

Violet nodded. "If you always come in this way, then you wouldn't have noticed the knight was missing right away since you didn't walk by it every day."

"Thank goodness." He tapped the side of his head. "I thought I was losing my marbles. Scarlett had convinced me that she was the clever Finch sister, but with that brilliant observation, I see the family resemblance is more than looks."

Violet snorted. "Most people assume that. And with Ruby holding a degree, and now the librarian, it's understandable to imagine I missed out on the smarts."

"No one thinks that," he insisted. "And if it comes to my attention that they do, I will strongly advise them otherwise."

That made her smile. "Thank you. By the way, I have some good news."

"Let's have coffee while you tell me."

"Only if I make it. You should be sitting down and taking things easy."

He slipped into a chair with something like relief. "The concussion does seem to have hit me hard," he admitted.

"You must listen to your body, Arthur." Violet bustled about the wonderful kitchen which had everything a keen baker could want. "I also brought you my new muffins to try. I hid them in the back of the kitchen so no one else got them before I left."

He blinked and looked away. "You're too kind, Violet."

She crossed the kitchen to place a hand on his arm. "My friends call me Vi."

"Oh." He looked up at her and as she suspected he was on the verge of tears.

"You have a beautiful kitchen," she told him brusquely.

"I built it for a beautiful lady."

He said this so softly she barely caught it, but she didn't respond. Someone else being in love with her mom didn't feel right, even now. Yet, as she opened cupboards and drawers, she could see her mom in here. Lilac Finch deserved a place to cook such as this and would have loved it.

When she placed the coffee and muffin in front of Arthur

he was once more in control. "The muffin looks wonderful. Is that the good news?"

She laughed. "Hopefully you like it, but that's not what I meant. I came to tell you about my trip."

He tutted. "How rude of me. You went to see your assessor friend not just for my sake. Was it everything you wanted it to be?"

"And so much more! Plus, Phin would like to come this weekend to check out your other pieces of interest if you agree."

"That is good news. I'd be happy to pay him for his time—however long it takes."

Violet hadn't considered it and spoke without doing so again. "I'm pretty sure he would do it for nothing as a favor to me. He was really interested in what you might have here."

"That's fine, but I need a professional and someone of his caliber should be paid."

Since she hadn't talked money with Phin, this seemed the best outcome. The two of them could haggle and leave her out of it. "Okay. I'll tell him."

"He can also stay here if that makes life easier. I have plenty of rooms and a bodyguard," he added wryly.

Violet chuckled. "That sounds perfect. Is Viktor staying too?"

"He is. Which should be interesting."

Violet chuckled. "Yes, he doesn't look like the sleepover kind of guy."

"He was in the army, so I guess he's used to close quarters and he'll have his own room and bathroom." Arthur smirked. "I sure wouldn't like to meet him in the dark and when he arrived soon after I did today, my heart nearly gave out."

Violet laughed. "I felt the same way when he turned up at our house with Alex, but he's rather sweet and interesting too."

"I haven't had much time with him because of the deputy asking questions, but I already agree. He is interesting, and eager to do a good job for me. Speaking of which, would you like to stay for dinner?"

"Thanks, but no. It's my turn to cook tonight so I need to get home."

"That would make anyone jealous. All you girls cook wonderfully."

She smiled at his sincerity. "Scarlett's the best hands down, but thanks to mom, Ruby and I do a passable job. Don't you have a cook anymore?"

He suddenly looked sheepish. "I've had a few, and in the past they left for reasons you can probably imagine. However, the last one just up and left the other day which was a shock as I'm pretty sure I was my least grumpy self. As far as I knew she had no job to go to and no family nearby."

Violet gasped. "Did you tell the sheriff this?"

"What do you mean?" He blinked. "He asked if I had staff, and I said no which is true."

"You should say something about it, Arthur. It could be relevant."

He considered this before nodding. "You're right. I'm a fool. She could know the thief."

Violet frowned. "It surprises me the sheriff didn't ask about who might have keys."

"He seemed to have a lot on his mind?"

"Well, that doesn't sound like him at all. I honestly think you should give him a call."

"I will. Just as soon as I finish this muffin."

"Good. Now, can I make you something before I go?"

"No, you run along. Viktor said he would rustle me up something, and though I have no idea what that means, he has to be better at it than me."

"I hear he can cook, so I think you're in safe hands all round."

He saw her to the door. "Thanks so much for looking out for the house. The sheriff told me all about last night and your part in things." He winked again. "And as for worrying about me—it's been a long time since someone did that and I must admit it is rather nice."

The pleasure and sadness in that comment touched her. Out of the blue, Violet kissed his cheek and then, red-faced, ran down the steps. Who was the more surprised out of the two of them she couldn't say. It was no more than a peck, but not so long ago, if someone had suggested that she might consider touching Arthur, let alone kiss him platonically, she'd have been horrified. Even now, she hoped he wouldn't mention it to anyone. She wasn't exactly known for being demonstrative with her emotions.

Unless it related to a mystery.

CHAPTER NINE

It was mid-morning the next day, when Ruby, George, and Bob suddenly peered in the open back door of the cafe. Scarlett and Violet were baking between a lull of serving customers and Olivia was at the craft store.

"Are you okay?" Ruby asked, breathing heavy, her face flushed,

"What do you mean and what are you doing here?" Scarlett asked, wiping her hands on her apron.

"Stay, good boys," Ruby told the pets on the doorstep. George turned his head in disgust, while Bob sat obediently, his nose twitching at the smells. "I tried to phone, but neither of you answered your mobiles. Alex phoned me to say that Viktor rang him and there's something going on at Arthur's."

The pan Violet was greasing slipped from her fingers and clattered to the floor. "Like what? And why are you here worrying about us?"

"There's been a sighting of a someone prowling around again. And of course, I thought of you, Vi." Ruby irritably pushed her blonde hair behind her ear. "It occurred to me that you might be there, and I wanted to check you weren't."

"Oh. I was planning on seeing him once we closed." Violet admitted. She ran to the window which didn't help at all. Arthur's house was also on Main Street and down the road a way and this window looked out to the parking lot. "I wonder what's happened. I never heard any sirens, so maybe Viktor scared him off."

"Do you think so?" Ruby hugged herself. "I hoped having Viktor would have deterred the thief from returning, but maybe it's made him more determined."

The doorbell jangled and Violet sighed. She had to put her shopkeeper face on, and she knew where she'd rather be. "The craft ladies are having a get together, slash party, here to celebrate purchasing their new shop."

"That seems a little premature since they haven't signed any papers yet, but have fun," Ruby teased. "I better get back to the library in case someone is trying to get in."

"Maybe you should stay here. You don't know where the person hanging around Arthur's is exactly," Scarlett suggested.

"They won't want anything at the library, and I'll run."

"Okay, but don't go near Arthur's," Scarlett warned.

"Of course not."

Violet called out on her way to the counter. "But if you do see anything from the road…"

"Vi, don't encourage her."

"Hello, is there any service today?" A woman's voice called from the café.

Scarlett grimaced at her hands which were once more full of the pastry she was kneading.

Violet sighed. "It's okay, I'm going."

"There you are. We were about to help ourselves," Leona Wolf chortled.

"Sorry, what can I get you?"

"I'll have a blueberry muffin and a latte."

"Make that two," Gail Norman called from the corner table.

Linda Night waved a hand. "I'll have the same, please."

Leona returned to the table and the women began chattering about anything and everything, not necessarily listening to each other.

Violet made the coffees, filled a tray with the cups and muffins, adding dishes of butter she knew they would ask for, and delivered them to the table.

"How is Arthur getting on with his new staff member?" Linda asked.

"Since he only started yesterday, we can assume he's not run out on him yet," Leona said snippily.

"Have you seen the man? He's huge." Gail licked her lips, and it wasn't clear if that was over the muffin or not.

Disgruntled, Violet nodded. "Viktor is a big man."

"I think I'll take a hotpot to Arthur tonight." Linda sighed. "He must be finding it hard now that Imogen's gone."

"From what I hear she didn't know her way around a kitchen too well." Leona sniffed disdainfully.

Intrigued, Violet pushed the sugar bowl closer. "Is that the mayor's last cook? Why did she leave?"

"Why do they all leave?" Gail smirked. "Our mayor isn't exactly a walk in the park."

"That was in the past. Arthur's different these days, isn't he?" Linda sighed again.

Gail frowned. "Why yes, he is. Still, Imogen couldn't handle all the work on her own. It's such a big place and she complained that the dusting alone took most of her time. He does have a lot of things in that house. Knickknacks and such from his ancestors. Maybe that's why she couldn't spend enough time on decent meals."

"She's a terrible cook. I don't know that more time would fix that," Leona added snarkily.

Linda gasped. "That's not a nice thing to say."

"I'm only repeating what she one day admitted to me."

Ignoring the other two, Violet moved the sugar bowl closer to Linda."You know her?"

"We're friends. Her husband was from around here too, but they moved to Destiny. She came back here looking for work. A live in housekeeper job suited her, but it didn't seem right to be there with just Arthur, so she commuted." Linda huffed. "It made for a very long day."

Violet shifted the subject slightly. "Have you been in his house recently?"

Linda snorted. "The mayor isn't one for impromptu visits and the last time he had a dinner party was when your mom was alive."

"So, no one ever gets inside his house these days?"

The women looked at each other questioningly and perhaps a little suspiciously. They all shook their heads.

"We have stopped by, but he doesn't want our help and doesn't seem to need any friends." Linda got a dreamy look in her eyes. "That might change now he's on medication for his meanness."

Violet bit back a laugh. Not that Arthur's past illness was amusing. It was that at least two of these women had their sights set on the mayor, and it clearly irked them that he wasn't interested.

"He certainly has changed his tune with you girls, so who knows how he might feel now," Gail added hopefully.

The door banged open, and Nate entered, breathing heavily just as Ruby had earlier. "Scarlett!" he yelled.

"Oh, my!" Leona yelped. "Is that really necessary right by my ear?"

Scarlett came running while without an apology Nate corralled the craft group to the back of the café with a good deal of fussing. Then he took Scarlett's hand for the briefest of moments. "Lock the doors and keep back from the windows. There's a gunman on the loose."

Violet gasped. "What about Ruby? She's probably all alone at the library."

He closed his eyes for a moment. "I'll see to her. Just stay inside and I'll be back when we have him in custody."

With that Nate ran back outside and just before the door closed, they heard a gunshot. Violet locked the door and ushered the frightened women behind the counter while Scarlett attended to the back door.

"Stay behind here," Violet told them firmly. There was hardly enough room for everyone and, though fearful, they didn't appreciate being told what to do, and might get antsy if stuck here for too long.

"Who do you think it is?" Leona whispered.

Linda peeked around the cabinet. "I don't know."

"Someone who has a gun."

Leona snorted. "Of course it is, Gail, but everyone in Cozy Hollow has one."

"I don't."

"Me either." Linda sniffed. "Who do you think he's after?"

Violet grimaced as Scarlett joined them. Naturally, they were all scared, but this was like herding chickens and would get tedious very fast.

"Where's Olivia?" Leona asked.

The sisters gasped and Scarlett pulled out her phone. Olivia answered on the first ring and Scarlett put her on speaker so Violet could hear.

"Are you okay?"

"I'm fine. You do remember I'm not coming in today except to drop by for coffee with the group?"

"Yes, but don't come. You should stay home and lock the doors until you hear different. There's someone running around town with a gun."

"Are you serious?"

"I wish I weren't. Didn't you hear the gunshot?"

"No, I just got out of the shower, and was blow-drying my hair until you phoned. Lucky I heard that. Now, tell me what's happening?"

"All I know is that someone just fired at least one shot. Make sure you're locked in, and I'll call when we hear from Nate, okay."

"Yes, dear. You all stay safe too."

Time seemed to be suspended as they waited. Violet was not the most patient of people, but the group were fussing like bees around a honeypot. Or in this case, the display cabinet.

"Who wants more coffee? On the house."

"What a good idea." Leona pursed her lips. "We didn't get to drink ours. Can we watch you make it with that monster of a machine? It fascinates me how you get so many different drinks from the same beans."

Violet wasn't sure how she could possibly stop them since they were almost standing on her feet, so the next while was taken up with her showing them how the 'fancy' machine worked.

"Is there something burning?"

"My cupcakes!" Scarlett ran into the kitchen, and they followed like sheep.

"What a lovely kitchen," Linda exclaimed. "It's much warmer and there's more room. Perhaps we should stay in here."

Violet shrugged at Scarlett. "I guess it's just as safe. No touching—for hygiene reason—and you can sit at the table well away from the window and door."

Clutching mugs of cappuccinos, they eagerly sat staring as if the sisters were about to provide a show.

Leona eyed the fresh cupcakes which Scarlett had barely

saved. "I didn't get to eat my muffin."

"Let them cool a little and I'll frost these for you. They're a little over done, but still edible."

"And free?"

Scarlett managed a less than sincere smile. "Naturally."

Violet smirked, as she made her way to the window. While the ladies thought they were getting special treatment, Scarlett had never sold anything less than perfect, so giving them away would always have been her intention.

Nothing moved outside and that meant that the gunman was on the loose somewhere. She trusted Nate to keep Ruby safe, but what about the rest of the residents? The ones who didn't know what was happening, like Olivia. There was an alarm that could be sounded in emergencies, yet it hadn't gone off which was odd.

She went back into the café as Nate appeared at the door and she ran to let him in—just as the siren sounded. Bob bounded in as well, his claws clicking on the floor, and he skidded to a stop in the middle of the room to bark loudly.

Bob knew he wasn't allowed in the cafe or the kitchen and this unusual behavior made her stomach clench, as did the look on Nate's face which told her his news wasn't good.

"Bob, be quiet. Right now, mister!" She put her hand up and he eased off to a rumbling growl. At least now she could hear herself think. "Nate, where is Ruby?"

"Ruby's gone," he stated somberly.

Her heart plummeted. "What do you mean, gone?"

"The library is empty."

"Maybe she went home."

He raised an eyebrow, but spoke gently. "Have you spoken to her?"

She shook her head and turned to face Scarlett whose face was pale as flour. "We have to find her."

"No, you have to stay in here and look after the others." Nate tapped his chest. "I'll find her."

"How can you promise that when you can't find the man with a gun?" Violet protested. "You haven't, have you?"

Scarlett pulled her into a hug. "We have to trust him."

Violet wasn't sure that she could, and Nate seemed aware of this.

"I'll call if—when I get any news."

"You better." Violet told him.

The craft ladies crowded in the doorway as he left followed by Bob who snuck out as quickly as he'd snuck in.

"What's happened?" Leona demanded.

Violet had forgotten about them, and once Scarlett gave them a break down, they were on fire with a barrage of questions. How could she wait here indefinitely listening to their conjecture while poor Ruby was...in trouble?

And what about Bob and George? They would never leave Ruby if she were in trouble. Her stomach clenched once more. Had Bob been trying to tell her something?

CHAPTER TEN

Every minute seemed an hour and Violet was at her wit's end. Scarlett was being so kind to the other women, while Violet had the urge to tell them to shut up with their never-ending questions about the criminal, Arthur, the sisters' love lives (just to change things up), and the progress on the diner.

She sidled up to Scarlett. "I have to do something."

"No, Vi. You heard what Nate said. We have to stay here."

"I can't."

Scarlett's lips pursed. "And I can't have two sisters out there in danger."

"I can find her, I know it."

Scarlett glared at her. "Like me, you have no idea where she is."

"Think about it. She'll have gone to find Alex."

Her sister's eyes widened briefly before she nodded. "Then she'll be safe. He would protect her with his life if necessary."

"I don't doubt that, but I want to make sure."

"Then phone him."

"Why didn't I think of that!" Violet pulled out her phone, angry with herself for missing the obvious. The two of them were guilty of putting their phones on silent while they worked so there were no distractions, and that's why Ruby couldn't get hold of them earlier. "I'll call Ruby. At least she picks up."

Scarlett blinked. "What idiots!"

Violet nodded and was about to key in the last digit when her finger hung mid-air. "Once Ruby heard the siren, if she had her phone, she'd be calling us to say she was safe and to check on us. I don't have any recent missed calls or messages. Do you?"

Scarlett checked and she paled again. "Nothing, and I turned the sound up. I think you're right and Ruby could be in a situation where her phone ringing could endanger her."

"Let me go find her. Please," Violet begged.

Scarlett shook her head vehemently. "No. I'll go."

Violet knew what her sister was thinking. They'd lost their mom, and now Ruby was in danger. Backing off and allowing Violet to take the lead in this was a lot to ask of Scarlett, but they were in the same position recently where Scarlett had gambled with her own safety. More than once. Violet took her hand. "It's my turn, Scarlett—to be the brave one."

There was a lengthy silence before Scarlett gulped. "You mean the stupid one."

Violet gave a tight smile. "That too."

"You better not get yourself killed."

"I'll do my very best." She kissed her sister's cheek and they walked to the back door arm in arm. "Lock up after me."

"Where are you going?" Linda stood fearfully in the middle of the room.

"It's okay. I'm just checking on Ruby. I'll be back soon.

Enjoy your cupcakes." Violet slid out the door and as soon as she heard the key turn, ran as fast as she could to the library, her head twisting left and right.

It wasn't far and she made a quick decision not to go in the front as it felt too conspicuous. She crept down the lane and up the back steps. Carefully easing the door open she paused to listen. Silence. Pulling the door closed behind her as quietly as possible, she pressed her back against the wall and tiptoed down the hall and into the restroom. It was empty, as was the lunchroom next to it, and the supply cupboard.

The small office looked that way too, but now her heart thumped impossibly harder. Scarlett had found the prior librarian dead behind the desk, so Violet's body and mind were reluctant to check. Steeling herself as much as a person could, she took the remaining steps forward and peered over the top of the worn wood to find the space behind...empty. She shuddered with relief.

That left the library itself.

Using the same caution, she stepped out into the open room. "Ruby?" Even softly spoken, her voice sounded loud in the high-ceilinged room. It wasn't a big library, but it was full of solid shelves which were crammed with books and four reading tables took up the only space except for the librarian's desk. Warily she checked behind each row of shelves. No Ruby. Was that good or bad?

Violet needed a new plan and her next stop had to be the nearly finished diner. Surely Ruby would make her way there. Hurrying to the front door she peeked out the window beside it. The street was still bare.

As she turned to go back the way she'd come, something caught her attention. Ruby's scarf, a bright floral number, hung from the shelf closest to the door as if it had caught on it. Did Ruby leave it behind deliberately?

A breeze gusted toward her, and she shivered. She hadn't thought to lock the back door and now someone was here. Heavy footsteps came down the hall and a man burst into the room before she could hide.

"Ruby?"

"Alex." His name came out in a strangled moan of relief.

"Violet! Where is she?" There was no mistaking the frantic tone.

"I don't know. I was on my way to find you. When she wasn't here, I hoped you'd both be at the diner looking over the rebuild, or you would know where she was." She gulped in air as if it had been cut off for too long.

He shook his head. "I haven't seen her. Nate already came by to check. I went to the café and Scarlett told me you were looking for her. I don't think that's a good idea. It would be better if I take you back there before I continue my search."

"If you're looking for Ruby, then I'm coming with you," she said stubbornly.

"I don't know…"

"She's my sister."

After a lengthy pause, he nodded. "We should check the mayor's place."

"Won't the sheriff be there by now?"

"He doesn't know the place like I do."

"What do you mean?"

"Viktor looked over every inch and he drew me a map of the house."

"Why would he do that?"

"Arthur wanted security and Viktor needed work while we wait for the diner to be ready to open, but he had a lot of time."

"I don't understand."

"I'll explain on the way."

Together they left the library and ran along the back of

the stores until they reached the walkway leading to Arthur's place. Violet tugged on his sleeve and he came to a sudden stop so that she bounced off him.

One strong arm held her upright and she leaned in to whisper. "Around here is a gap in the hedge."

"Are you sure? It's very thick."

"The man who was stealing from Arthur broke through from the other side. I don't know where he came out, but this looks about the right place if I think about where Arthur's driveway ends near the back garden."

Alex pushed aside a couple of branches and she pointed. "There. See how these bits are broken?"

He was such a big man, which meant he had to duck to get under the lowest branches, and Alex broke several more to fit through sideways. It was risky because of the noise, but necessary, and also made it a good deal easier for Violet to follow. He stopped before they walked out the other side onto the drive and she caught sight of the house.

A banging sound came from ahead of them.

"What's that?" she hissed.

He stood on tiptoe. "The back door is open and blowing in the wind. I can't see the police nearby, but it looks like there's something over by the window."

"Shall we go that way and see what it is?"

"I'll go first. Wait here until I signal it's okay." Considering his size, Alex ran light-footed across the gravel and, like a ninja, leaped onto the patio to come to a sudden stop by the door.

For a moment he stared at whatever he'd found, then he groaned and dropped to his knees.

Had he been shot? No, she would have heard that. She couldn't see his face, and it seemed like he'd forgotten about her. Not sure what the problem was, Violet took the fact that he wasn't doing anything but looking down as a sign that he wasn't in danger.

Heart hammering, she followed the path he'd taken, unaware until she was almost beside him, that due to a breeze, the door was banging gently on the wall and then back again to hit—a body.

CHAPTER ELEVEN

A red stain on the back of Viktor's jacket didn't bode well. His right cheek pressed against the concrete as he stared out to the garden. Another animal-like groan came from Alex, his fingers at Viktor's throat. He moved them several times around Viktor's neck and on his wrist to no avail and Alex's chin dropped to his chest in resignation.

Violet put a hand on his shoulder and squeezed gently. "I'm so sorry, Alex."

He nodded slowly and the face he turned to her was unrecognizable. "Not as sorry as the person who did this will be when I find them."

She felt the anger and sorrow buzzing through him as if searching for an outlet and a new fear gripped her. "I understand you're upset, but we can't do anything rash right now. The killer has a gun, and we don't."

"Upset doesn't scratch the surface and I don't need a gun," he growled.

Until then, Violet didn't think she could be any more frightened. Alex was understandably furious and that was never good when faced with criminals—murderers in particular. She should know after the trouble they'd had in the last year. She recognized that fear and anger she'd experienced when she thought Scarlett might be the victim of a warped mind. It had been almost too much to bear. It would be awful if Alex met the same fate as Viktor because anger clouded his judgement.

"What about Ruby?" She demanded. "If they killed you, what would stop them from hurting her?"

His eyes cleared a little as he considered this. "The sheriff and his deputies will take care of you all."

"Maybe, but Ruby would be devastated if something happened to you."

He blinked. "Would she?"

Finally, he had something to take the focus off revenge, and Violet didn't give him time to think of another reason to rashly go after the killer. "You know she would. She cares about you a great deal. I don't know where the sheriff and his men are, but we can't disturb the scene any more than we have. Although, we should check that Arthur is okay."

Alex hesitated, his hand still on Viktor. Then he straightened his shoulders and reached into his shirt pocket to pull out a bandana which he shook out and placed across his friends' face. Jerkily he stood. "You should wait out here."

"I'd rather be with you than out here alone," she protested.

Reluctantly, he nodded. "We don't know that the killer isn't inside, so stay behind me."

She didn't need more encouragement to do that, but before they went in she pushed a small planter in the way to stop the door hitting Viktor.

"Thank you," Alex said softly, then using himself as a shield, he eased inside.

Violet followed so close she couldn't see anything beyond him. The kitchen appeared to be empty, but as they crept down the hall items dotted the floor. It appeared as if someone had been carrying Arthur's things and suddenly dropped them. She thought of Viktor and the way he had fallen. Shot in the back, it was possible that he had chased the thief and, when they'd made a stand with gun in hand, he'd tried to get away.

She shook her head at the mental image. It wouldn't be a good idea to let her mind wander, or make assumptions about the thief leaving the scene and not coming back inside once he'd dealt with Viktor, but since the items were left behind, it made sense.

The trail of goods led to the study, so it was no surprise to find the trunk open and mostly empty. They checked behind the desk and found the drawers had been opened and papers strewn on the carpet.

"Do you think they got away with the most valuable items, or did Viktor stop them in time?" Violet wondered aloud.

"He would have done his very best," Alex stated flatly. "I guess you could check your list to see if anything's missing."

Before she could reply she heard footsteps. "Whoever is in there better come out with their hands up!" A voice bellowed from the hall.

"Nate, it's us, Violet and Alex." Her voice squeaked in relief and next minute Nate was at the door looking very annoyed.

"Before you say anything about us being here, I was worried about Ruby, and I was right to be. She's been taken."

He grimaced. "I know."

"What? And you didn't think to tell us?"

"There wasn't time for that." He growled. "I've been chasing the perpetrator all over town and I don't have enough men to pass messages."

If she was in her right mind, she would know he was

doing his best, but all she could think of was that Ruby was gone and with Nate's admission, probably for longer than she'd first thought. "Viktor is dead, but I guess you also knew that before now."

He flinched at her icy tone. "We did get here quickly after that shot, and this was how we found the scene. It's my job to find the guilty party as fast as possible and protect the living at the scene." Turning to Alex his voice softened. "The paramedics are waiting to come get Viktor. Like I said, he was dead by the time we found him, and I couldn't jeopardize their safety."

"I understand." Alex narrowed his eyes. "Viktor would want us to find this man and not be concerned about being out there alone in the cold."

Nate grimaced again, clearly not wanting to think about that, and Violet wrapped her arms around herself as goosebumps ran along her body. No one was safe, but what about the mayor?

"Where is Arthur?"

"He wasn't here before, but I'll have another look in case he came home." Nate ran lightly up the stairs while Alex went the other way.

Violet wasn't sure what to do, but clearly he had a plan. "What are you doing?"

"I told you that Viktor knows some secrets about the house," Alex called over his shoulder. "I will check that Arthur is not hiding in a place the murderer wouldn't know about."

Astonished, Violet trailed after him as he went into a reception room almost opposite the study. There was a heavy dresser with decanters and crystal glasses sitting on a marble top and a mirror affixed to the back. Alex ran his fingers around it and grunted his disgust at not finding anything.

This was intriguing. "Are you looking for a hidden opening? For a person to get through, it would need to be bigger than that dresser to conceal it."

"You are right." He grunted, then crouched to feel around the skirting boards. "All I know is there is a hidden button on wood near the dresser."

His frustration was catching, and she heard Nate on the stairs. Joining Alex at the dresser, her fingers danced across the wood edges like she was pushing keys on a typewriter, while her eyes scoped out the wall around it. Deep panels covered three of the walls to window height, while on this wall they went to the ceiling.

Violet moved her search to the edge of the first panel and at head-height she found a small bump. At first she dismissed it, but it was an anomaly to the rest of the smooth wood and her fingers were drawn back a couple of times.

Just before Nate found them, she pushed the area firmly and something clicked. Forcing her fingers into a small opening, she pulled with all her might—and the paneling with the dresser moved forward the smallest of fractions.

"You found it!" Alex cried and tugged it open the rest of the way. "This is ingenious. The mechanism is made as a counter weight and requires little strength."

"I wouldn't say that exactly," Violet objected.

"What the heck are you two doing?" Nate demanded.

"Checking that Arthur is not hiding here." Violet went inside the cavity full of hope, but that soon went. "Unfortunately, it's empty."

Nate came to check, but there wasn't enough room for the two of them. "How did you know about it."

"Viktor," Alex told him flatly.

"What do we do now?" Violet asked.

"Alex, would you take Violet back to the café?" the sheriff asked. "I need to locate my deputies."

"After that I will come find you," Alex told him stubbornly. "I want to help."

Nate shook his head. "I have no idea how this is going to go down. The murderer could have left town, but you should stay at the café to keep them safe until I give the all clear."

Strong emotions flittered across Alex's face. Obviously torn between what he really wanted to do and what was asked of him, it seemed his sense of honor was too strong to ignore. "Come, I will look after you and Scarlett. Ruby would want that."

The big Russian snatched at a comforter hanging over the buttoned chair and led the way to the back door. He gently placed the blanket over Viktor, saying something she couldn't understand, then continued down the steps to the gravel.

CHAPTER TWELVE

Silently they headed back to the café, keeping watch around them. There was no doubt Violet felt safer with Alex than if she were on her own, but as they got closer the situation hit her hard. How would she tell Scarlett that Ruby was still missing?

When they arrived at the parking lot behind the café, Scarlett was watching at the window. Their eyes met through the pane for a telling moment before Scarlett moved away and the door was yanked open.

"Where is she!"

Violet didn't realize she was crying until a fat tear dropped onto her jacket. "We don't know. She was gone when we got to the library."

Scarlett threw her arms around Violet, but Alex gave them no time to comfort each other and bundled them both inside.

"Tell me what happened," Scarlett demanded as soon as the door was locked.

Violet was incapable of speaking, so Alex had to deliver the whole story and both sisters were crying now as well as the craft ladies who huddled together by the table. Violet hadn't given them a thought and as soon as Alex finished the room erupted.

"Do you think he'll kill her?" Leona asked with a hiccup.

Gail gasped. "Why would he do that to our sweet Ruby?"

"It's not right." Linda moaned. "That girl wouldn't hurt a fly!"

"That's enough!" Scarlett shouted and the room stilled immediately.

Violet had never loved her more. Having witnesses to their distress was too much to deal with, especially when, no matter how unwittingly, the women added to it. If she could have run home and hidden in her room, she would have. She shook her head at the notion. This wasn't true. Instead she would be out scouring the town for their baby sister.

Alex, his face still ashen, paced the kitchen, then the café. He peered through windows and glanced frequently at the women. It was clear to Violet that he did not want to be here, and she totally empathized. Meanwhile Scarlett withdrew into herself and stared out the kitchen window.

Violet grew desperate for something to do so she wouldn't have to listen to the three women mumbling in the corner about Ruby's chances of being found. Making strong coffee was better than baking which was pointless right now, with no one to eat the food except the six people here.

She took a mug to her sister and held it out to her. "I'm sorry I didn't find Ruby."

Scarlett threw her arms around her and held on tight. "I know you did your best, and I don't blame you for any of this. I know how your mind works because mine went down the same track. We feel responsible for Ruby—for each other. If we accept that she was taken we must trust that Nate and his deputies will find her."

The tears fell again as they cried in each other's arms but

having a private moment couldn't last long. Not with four pairs of eyes watching their every move. And the anguish on Alex's face got more pronounced as if he were about to explode.

"What do we do with them?" Violet gestured to the group that sat at the table.

"To be honest, I've had some uncharitable thoughts, but they don't mean any harm."

Violet snorted. "Yeah, but they can't be silent for more than a minute."

"I think you'll find it's been much longer than that, dear."

Violet swung around to find Linda behind them white-knuckling her mug. "I thought you were hard of hearing, Mrs. Night?"

"Some days are better than others. I believe it depends on the acoustics."

Gail tittered. "Linda likes to pretend she's hard of hearing so she can eavesdrop."

"That is an outright lie." Linda huffed. "My hearing comes and goes. Which is ideal when people blather on about nothing worth listening to."

"Rude." Gail's chin trembled.

Leona strode across the room with purpose. "I don't think we should be arguing. It's up to us to make a plan to get Ruby home safe and sound."

"Who do you mean—*us*?" Gail squeaked.

"Why not us?"

"Because we're women of a certain age, Leona."

"I can't believe you said that. Haven't you always made out that we're just as good as men?"

Gail tapped her head. "Up here we are, if not better, but I can't imagine any of us in hand-to-hand combat."

"Then it's simple, we use our heads."

A glimmer of hope flickered through the gloom and Violet nodded enthusiastically. "Mrs. Wolf is right."

"Violet, don't encourage them," Scarlett pleaded. "I can't handle it right now."

"I know it doesn't sound feasible, but just listen. Everyone is locked down at home or their place of work, right?"

"I guess so."

"And they'll all be scared and twiddling their thumbs waiting for news. What if we use our phones and call everyone we know? If they can see around town and report on it, we can get a good idea of where the killer isn't."

"And that would narrow it down to where he could be," Alex said from the doorway with a measure of tempered excitement. "Or where Ruby is."

Appreciating his support, she managed a smile. "Exactly."

"This is a very good plan," he told Leona.

She puffed up like popcorn. "Well, it sure beats sitting here doing nothing."

"I don't have a phone, dear."

Violet stood in the middle of the room ready to spring into action at any chance. "That's okay, Mrs. Night. Whoever doesn't have a phone can take down names of people we have contacted so we don't all ring the same people."

Scarlett, suddenly getting a burst of adrenaline which seemed to be catching, pulled out paper and pens from the small desk in the corner. She slapped them on the table. "Let's start with those who can see over main street and especially across to the library—front and back."

Having something to do gave the group purpose and they responded in a lively way to the challenge. Violet also checked her phone for numbers they might not have. It didn't take long as she wasn't on as friendly terms with the townsfolk as either of her sisters.

She took a clean piece of paper and wrote down every

street she'd used since she left the café. Again, it was a short list. She'd been near the library, along the back of the shops, and then to Arthur's place. Alex had also come the whole of Main Street to get to the library and then the café. Neither had seen anyone else other than Nate and two of his deputies.

If the killer had gotten away, where would he take Ruby? And would he return for Arthur's possessions? The only way this made sense was if he intended to ask for a ransom because he had to leave behind the stolen goods. Or would he swap Ruby for all the goods or something specific?

Whatever the killer's intention, they needed to find Arthur in a hurry. He was the only one they knew with a decent amount of money to pay any kind of ransom. Plus, by the way he'd taunted him, it was highly likely the killer wanted the mayor to be the one to pay. But where did Arthur go—and why?

Her stomach churned. If the call came through for a ransom and they couldn't supply it, what would that mean for Ruby?

CHAPTER THIRTEEN

Gail and Leona's phones were surprisingly of decent quality and had full batteries. With Scarlett's list of questions they got onto the task with exuberance and a sense of importance. The town would never hear the end of this, Violet mused, grateful to the women for their willingness and, as it turned out, their extensive collection of phone numbers.

Every person they called was anxious and all wanted to feel useful, while gleaning as much information as the women would give them time for. They checked every window in their houses and each aspect they could see from them. They were also asked for an account of where they were when the gunfire sounded and what happened next around them. It was a long shot that they'd caught sight of the killer, but he couldn't disappear into thin air. Especially if he had Ruby with him.

That last thought made Violet sick to her stomach, but she perked up when Scarlett's excited voice drew her attention.

"You saw Bob?" she spoke loudly into her mobile.

"Where?" Violet mouthed.

"Scratching at the storm shelter behind the library? Thank you! That's a great help." Scarlett ended the call, her eyes shining with hope.

"I will go now and check." Alex was already by the door.

"Not without me you won't." Violet gave Scarlett an apologetic glance, but for once her sister didn't argue and she was out the door before anyone could stop her.

Alex gave her a hard look from the bottom step, as if he would refuse to let her come, but she matched his look and he must have decided against that, so her resolve wasn't tested. She had failed to search everywhere, and this was her chance to rectify that. Violet gulped. *If they were in time.*

He motioned with his head and soon they were racing across the parking lot again, while Scarlett locked up behind them, and no doubt called Nate.

This time they took the back way to the library, heading straight for the storm shelter. It was over grown and as they arrived, Bob came scrambling out from under a shrub. He whined at Violet and then the door, which was old, but looked solid enough. The wood that usually kept the door closed by sliding into brackets on either side was missing. Which meant that it was possibly in the brackets inside. Adding grass which had been pulled from the ground around the front edge to the missing brackets and Bob still being here, these were clues that couldn't be ignored.

Alex crouched a few feet away from the shelter and when Bob whined, she followed suit.

Attempting to keep her excitement in check, Violet whispered to Alex. "We could call her name, but what if he's in there with her waiting for things to die down?"

"The sheriff doesn't think he's hanging around town, but as much as I agree that this person doesn't want to be caught, which is more likely to occur if he stayed just to capture Ruby, it doesn't mean he left."

He looked around him and reached out to pick up a heavy stick, a potential weapon, which seemed reinforce what he'd just said.

"Maybe we don't know for sure that the killer is inside, but I think Ruby is, and so does Bob. This person isn't in their right mind, and I don't think we should wait any longer. We have to consider Ruby is in there on her own, possibly injured, and that she escaped the killer who is long gone."

Frowning, Alex scanned around them once more. "Perhaps, but even if he isn't in there, we can't be sure he is not watching."

Now she was confused. "Okay, he might still be in town, but you don't think he's in the shelter?"

He nodded. "That is my gut feeling."

"He left behind all the treasures because he was caught, and probably killed Viktor because he wants them so desperately." Violet groaned with anguish. "He will try again."

Alex stood decisively. "You are right. We must get Ruby out of there. The place is old, decaying and she will be freezing." He grimaced as if the idea was intolerable and crept forward.

She followed on his heels. Just because she thought the killer wasn't inside, didn't mean she wasn't scared, and she jumped when he spoke much louder than before.

"Ruby, are you in there?" His big hand twitched over where the door met in the middle. He tried to pry them open, but they barely budged.

"Alex? Is that you?"

Ruby's sweet voice made them grin at each other.

"Yes, it is me. Open the door, please."

"Are you alone?"

"Violet is here too."

They heard her grunt as she lifted the wood and when he heard it fall to the ground, Alex immediately yanked open the heavy door. Ruby emerged into the watery sunlight like a princess awakened and he folded her into his arms. George sauntered out after her to wrap himself around Violet's legs while Bob danced around them yipping.

"I should have known you'd have a bodyguard," Violet chuckled and joined the hug.

The sound of shoes on gravel had Alex thrust Ruby behind him a split second before Nate and Deputy Glasson rounded the corner guns at the ready. They skidded to a halt, surprise and relief plastered on their faces.

"How did you find her?" Nate asked.

"The town did. The craft ladies in particular," Violet told him proudly.

"What am I going to do with you, Violet Finch?"

"Well, I don't know about you, but I need coffee. I must have made a dozen cups today and not drunk a single one."

"Am I allowed out or have you forgotten about me?" A man stepped from the shelter and into the light, calmly brushing dust off his jacket.

"Arthur," Violet squealed. "You're alive."

"Last time I checked," he mused. "Is everyone else safe?"

Alex made a desperate sound and looked away.

"What's happened?" Ruby was immediately concerned and tried to get him to look at her.

"Look there's a lot to talk about, but let's get inside the café, so we're all together." Nate didn't wait for agreement and led the way back, gun kept at the ready and still on the alert in case the killer showed up.

The situation was unnerving, and though Ruby and Arthur were safe, Violet had momentarily forgotten Viktor, which wasn't right. As they hurried to the café she caught the look of sadness and shame on Alex's face as if he too had forgotten about his friend.

Her mind raced. How did Arthur make his way to Ruby, and why there and not the Sheriff's office? And when did he do that? Before or after Viktor died? She barely knew Viktor, but if Alex valued him so highly as a friend, then she trusted that the man had taken his job seriously and put himself in harm's way to protect Arthur. The way Viktor died was horrible enough, but to Alex it must be doubly hard to accept. As yet he'd had no time to mourn, and it likely wouldn't happen until they caught the killer. Would Alex take it into his own hands to seek justice if Nate didn't find the killer?

Her head was spinning by the time they reached the café. Nate told Deputy Pine to check on the roadblocks on the main roads in and out of town, and Scarlett already had the door unlocked.

She pulled Ruby into her arms. "Thank goodness. I don't think I could have waited much longer."

Ruby sniffed into her shoulder, and they moved into the room. The craft group went crazy congratulating the rescuers, and there was much hugging and chatter.

Not much of a hugger, unless it was her sisters or Aunt Olivia, Violet extricated herself to make coffee—again—while Scarlett wrapped the frozen Ruby in blankets and the craft group attended to Arthur. Much to his awkward frustration.

"Please, I'm fine." He pushed gently at their hands as they fought to be the one to give him comfort.

It truly looked like mutiny was about to ensue. Luckily, Nate forced his way between them and the mayor like a human shield. "Give the man some air," he said gruffly.

That didn't go down well.

"We're just trying to help!" Leona exclaimed.

Gail tsked. "He's as cold as ice, poor love."

"He could have hypothermia. You should have got to him sooner," Leona added sourly.

"Now, now," Ruby said soothingly. "The sheriff is just trying to do his job and our mayor can't tell his side of things if you're asking him questions." She smiled at each of them. "No matter how well meaning."

Violet had to admire the way her youngest sister dealt with people, by appealing to the best part of them, in that encouraging way she had. It left a person unable to take offence and Ruby accepted this as normal rather than the talent it so obviously was.

"Everyone helped," Scarlett agreed. "The town came together to find Ruby and we're so grateful to every single person who took the time to look. And finding Ruby led to the mayor, so well-done ladies—you make a great team!"

The women preened and Nate made a statement.

"As Ruby stated, you've done a fantastic job which won't be forgotten, but we still have questions of our own to ask and a criminal to find. If you ladies could all be patient a while longer I'd appreciate it a great deal."

The group puffed up like choux pastry and finally simmered down.

Violet smirked while she poured coffees. These ladies were all about a good story, and if it included them, so much the better.

CHAPTER FOURTEEN

"Can you talk us through what happened?" Nate pulled up a chair in front of Ruby who had curled up on the small sofa tucked into the corner of the room. Arthur sat beside her and gratefully accepted the cup of coffee Violet handed him. He took a long sip of the hot liquid and closed his eyes for a moment.

By the time he opened them, the craft group surrounded them, focused as one on his tale, and they weren't the only ones.

He grimaced. "Perhaps you should go first, Ruby."

Ruby's mouth quivered and Violet took a step toward her, intending to sit next to her for encouragement, but Alex was quicker and he squeezed into the space beside Ruby, his head bent at an odd angle against the low point of the ceiling.

Ruby gave him a watery smile and took a deep breath. "I was shelving books by the front door when something outside the window caught my attention. You can imagine my shock when I saw a man crouched with a gun running along the store fronts across Main Street. Fortunately I was alone, so I locked the front door, but I think he heard me because when I looked out the window again, he was crossing the street, tucking the gun inside his jacket and headed toward the library." She stopped for a moment and licked her lips.

Violet quickly handed her a glass of water.

Taking a long drink, Ruby wiped her mouth on the back of her hand. "The library may have brick walls, but the back door is rickety, so I didn't feel safe. With no suitable place to hide inside I ran out the back and almost had a heart attack when Arthur came flying around the corner. We were both terrified and there wasn't time to go into details with each other, or think of somewhere better to hide, so I decided the shelter was a good idea and close enough to reach in case the gunman had tried the front door and was already on his way around the back. I should add that George was sitting on the shelter doors, so it seemed like a sign."

Leona gasped when Ruby called the mayor Arthur, but no one paid her much attention since the rest of them were caught up in the story.

"Once inside, and we'd managed to secure the wood in the brackets, we thought we heard footsteps coming closer. It was terrifying, but then Bob started barking and I guess it frightened him away. To be honest we were beginning to wonder if anyone would come for us." She looked up at Alex with adoration. "Which I can see was a silly notion."

Nate coughed, pulling them out of the story. "All right, thank you Ruby. Mayor Tully, what happened prior to that?"

Arthur sighed heavily. "Being stuck at home for my own safety, felt like I was in prison, so when Viktor offered to cook tonight, I went with him to get supplies." He put a hand up to Nate. "I know what you're thinking, but it was daylight —and have you seen the size of Viktor?"

Nate looked unimpressed but nodded. "Go on."

"We got to the front door when we heard a crash from

around the back of the house. Viktor told me to get out of there while he went to check it out. I got as far as the road when I heard a gunshot and then I ran to the sheriff's office. I admit I was plenty worked up when I got there and told Deputy Glasson what I knew. He explained that the sheriff wasn't in, and the protocol was to sound the disaster warning siren. He told me to stay there, and he would lock me in because he had to find the sheriff, but all I could think of was the fright Ruby would get when she heard it. I had to check if she was okay, so I refused his offer."

The sheepish look he gave everyone spoke of just where Ruby sat in his esteem. She blushed, but no one commented as they waited for him to continue.

"The siren was so loud and even though I'd been warned, it made me more afraid than before. I snuck around the back of the stores until I got to the library and that's when I ran into Ruby who hurriedly explained about the gunman, and I agreed that the shelter was the only place close enough to get to before he found us."

Nate had looked thoughtful while Arthur told his story and now he shook his head. "Are you saying the gunman wasn't chasing you?"

"I don't rightly know." Arthur scratched his head. "Was he ever truly after me, or what was inside my house?"

Violet had an epiphany which she blurted out. "He must have been watching the place to know that neither of you were home and took the opportunity to get his hands on what he wanted all along. Whatever that is. Then he probably heard Viktor coming around the side of the house and hid."

"What makes you say that?" Arthur asked.

Violet gave Alex an apologetic look for discussing Viktor's demise this way. "By the time Alex and I got there, things were strewn along your hall leading to the back door. It seems poor Viktor ran into an ambush."

"What are you talking about?" Arthur demanded. "The gunman was running around town, so we should assume Viktor scared the thief off."

"But you heard the gunshot…oh, no." Violet bit her lip. Arthur clearly had no idea that Viktor was dead.

A hiss escaped from Alex.

Nate sat a little straighter and spared her having to spill the news. "Viktor was shot at the rear of your house. I'm afraid he's dead."

A collective gasp rang out and Alex paled. Ruby clutched his hand, her eyes welling.

"What? No!" Arthur shook his head. "That can't be right."

"I'm so sorry to tell you that I saw Viktor, and it is the truth," Nate said sadly.

Violet swallowed hard. "Something in your house is so important to the thief that they've resorted to murder. We need to know what that is."

"For Viktor's sake you must tell us," Alex pleaded. "He can't have died for nothing."

Arthur blanched. "I swear, I have no idea. If I did, I would tell you."

"Of course you would, Mayor," Linda spoke in earnest.

Arthur ignored her and continued to address Alex. "I've spent weeks going through everything in the house trying to figure out what would be worth repeated attempts to steal it."

"And?"

"Nothing stands out. I have some nice pieces, but on their own they're not worth that much."

"I wonder what he wanted in the library?" Violet muttered.

Nate turned. "What do you mean?"

"It occurred to me more than once that if he just killed a man you'd think he'd want to high tail it out of town. Especially once the siren sounded to alert every citizen. Instead, he went to the library. If he didn't know where the mayor had gone, and judging by the time frame, he couldn't have, why go there?"

"Hmmm." Nate scratched his head. "That's an interesting angle."

"These girls are so clever," Gail stage whispered.

Nate's mouth twisted unhappily. "So, what could be in the library that was so important he didn't leave town?"

"From what Alex and I saw, he was escaping with some loot when Viktor appeared. Maybe he found a clue while he was rifling through Arthur's stuff."

"A clue to what?"

Nate wasn't the only one frowning and Violet wished she'd kept quiet. *Too late now.*

"I don't know, but what if we check all those things strewn around Arthur's place? The killer was in such a hurry to get away I imagine he didn't get back there to collect them. Maybe there is a clue among those items that would explain why he went to the library."

Nate considered this and nodded. "Two of my deputies have staked the place out and I'd like to have a look around anyway." He stood and so did everyone else in the room. The group buzzed around Arthur and again the sheriff intervened. "You ladies have heard far more than you should, so I'm going to ask you to keep this to yourselves for now. Alex would you mind escorting them home?"

"Do you think that's wise?" Gail asked fearfully.

"I am reasonably satisfied that the only people in danger are Arthur and anyone connected to his property."

"But what if you're wrong and he is still out there?" Leona asked indignantly.

"I will make sure you are safe," Alex told her firmly. He sent Ruby an apologetic glance as he stoically accepted the task given him and began to usher the reluctant group through to the café.

"Could we get something to take home?" Linda suggested. "I don't think I'll be up to cooking tonight, and we've only had a cupcake all afternoon."

Scarlett joined the line. "I'll bag you each a muffin or a pastie to take with you. On the house."

Though not entirely, that perked them up a bit. Plus, they had so much fodder for gossip, Violet would bet as soon as they felt safe they would meet up at one of their houses to dissect every moment of the ordeal. "I'm glad someone enjoyed their day," she muttered.

Ruby tutted. "They did a good job with the phone calls, and it was better that they were here safe and not scared to death in their homes."

"That's why they love you." Violet sighed. "What can I say? I was scared for you. We all were, and they did help us find you. While that turned out okay, Viktor is still dead. She turned to Nate who was speaking to his deputy. "I'm ready when you are, Sheriff."

Ruby's small fists clenched. "Me too. If this is connected to the library you'll need my expertise."

Nate was at the back door. "I've been thinking that it's too dangerous to bring you. Arthur will have a fair idea now that he has a list and if necessary, I'll come back and get you or bring items to you."

"You might not see the relevance of what was taken and what he discarded." Violet stated firmly. "Plus, that will take so much longer if you have to keep coming back here. Do we really have the time to muck around?"

He groaned, then wagged a finger at her. "At the first sign of trouble you will do as I say. Make that as soon as we leave here."

The sisters nodded effusively until they caught sight of Scarlett tapping her foot in the entranceway behind them.

"I knew you'd get involved as soon as my back was turned. I'm not happy about it, but as usual you'll both do what you want. Just don't do anything stupid."

Her heated words barely concealed her worry and there was an awkward moment between the three of them.

Nate grimaced. "I'll take care of Ruby and Violet."

"I'll hold you to that, Sheriff." Scarlett turned stiffly away from the group.

"If you could send Alex our way for backup when he returns, I'd appreciate it."

"Of course, Sheriff."

Deputy Glasson, who was stationed outside the back door, bookended the sisters and Arthur with Nate on the other side of them, and they hurried down the street to the Mayor's house. Arthur looked exhausted, while Violet could feel Ruby trembling.

"She'll get over it if we stay safe, Rubes."

"Well, I intend to, what about you?"

Violet was a little taken aback by her sister's sarcasm. "Don't start on me. We need to stick together."

Ruby tilted her head. "Like a team?"

"Sure."

"The problem with that is, you're not exactly a team player."

"Hey, I wasn't the first one to leave the café."

"Ouch! Go ahead and tell me how you really feel."

Ruby moved closer to Nate, leaving Violet to walk beside Deputy Glasson, who was keeping his eyes peeled, and not interested in sisterly spats. She shouldn't have said that, but were they really arguing about the café, or was this about Ruby's guilt at ignoring Scarlett? Or her worry for Alex after losing his friend.

Violet sighed. It seemed the whole of Cozy Hollow was feeling tetchy these days, but she had other things on her mind right now. The list of items began to run through her mind and along with that came a much-needed shot of adrenaline.

CHAPTER FIFTEEN

In a horrible sense of deja vu, Deputy Pine was stationed at the front door and tape ran once more around the path and front veranda. When he saw the sheriff he stiffened and looked on the verge of saluting.

"The ambulance and paramedics are around the back with the deceased, sir. I said they could remove the body now that all the photos have been taken. I hope that was okay?"

"Yes, that's fine. Just keep everyone else outside and keep a close watch on that hedge line." Nate pointed down the driveway to where, thanks to Alex, the gap was now significantly larger.

"Yes, Sir."

Nate lifted the tape to allow the others to get inside. From his pocket he handed the women a pair of gloves each. "Don't move anything and be careful where you step."

"What about me," Arthur asked.

"We'll assume that your fingerprints are already on most, if not all of the items, so you don't need gloves, but I'd still rather none of you touch anything that isn't necessary."

They followed him down the hall, and though they could see where the trail began, their first stop was Arthur's study. The chest was empty. A few things were dotted around it, but nothing that looked expensive.

"What do you think?" Violet asked her sister and Ruby shrugged.

"Nothing stands out to me. Come on, let's look at the rest."

There was a small pile of loot in the doorway leading into the kitchen which they stepped delicately over.

"This must be where he was when the killer heard you arrive home, Arthur," Violet mused. "They've dropped the pile in a hurry and some of the items have spilled off it and rolled further away."

"It troubles me that you're so certain," Nate told her as he knelt to inspect a brooch.

"It's only science that makes me think that's what happened, and I could be wrong." Violet said automatically as she caught sight of a book smaller than her hand. It looked very old. "I want to look closer at this, Sheriff."

He came back to her, and they knelt together, heads almost touching. "What is it?"

"That's an old ration book." Arthur peered over their shoulders. "It was my grandmother's."

Nate pulled out a pair of tweezers and lifted the book gently, placing it in Violet's gloved hands.

Inside the first page was written "United States of America War Ration Book One, followed by a warning message about the misuse of it and there was a serial number. The next pages were Arthur's grandmother's details, signature, and serrated edges where stamps must have been. The serial number was repeated on each page as was the title reading, "Office of Price Administration."

"I've heard of these, but never seen one," Violet said excitedly.

"We have a couple in the library," Ruby noted.

"Really?"

"Since we don't have a museum. Locals often donate things we might be interested in, and which don't take up too much space."

Nate scratched his head. "I can't see how this would be important to the thief."

"People don't always steal for monetary gain," Violet reminded him.

"That is true. Maybe we should consider Arthur's history."

Ruby's eyes lit up. "I was just about to suggest that."

"You've completely lost me," Arthur sighed his exasperation.

"While these possessions are interesting, I honestly can't see anything here that makes me think money is the real objective. I'm suggesting that the thief wants something you have which means more to them than money."

"And you'll find out what that is by looking at my history?"

"Potentially. They might think they have a right to whatever it is."

"A ration book? Why would they have rights to that, and what about everything else?"

"They probably don't want the ration book, but maybe they think that by stealing a lot it will hide the truth of what they really want."

"Sounds like a lot of maybes to me." Nate interrupted. "Look, I want to have another check over the scene once they take Viktor away. You should go with Deputy Pine and I'll instruct him to take you back to the library or the café."

"Can I look over Arthurs' stuff a while longer before we go?" Violet almost begged.

Nate huffed out a long breath. "Okay, but don't move anything. Photos have been taken in here, but I need the items to stay put a while longer."

"Thank you and we won't move a thing."

He gave her the side-eye and went to the back door, opening it carefully. The three of them watched Nate step to the right and got a glimpse of the top of Viktor before the door was shut firmly.

Ruby sniffed. "I hadn't wanted to truly believe it, Vi."

"I know." Violet gave her a hug. "It's so sad he's gone."

"He was a little scary when you first met him, but according to Alex, was the sweetest man." Ruby gulped. "Poor Alex is distraught at losing his best friend. He never had one before Viktor and they kept in touch the whole time when Alex moved here. Then Alex saved enough money and arranged a job before he sent for Viktor and helped him deal with all the paperwork."

"Let's try not to think about it until we've solved this," Violet said gently.

"I don't mean to be rude, but if the sheriff can't sort out this mess, how do you propose to do it?" Arthur was looking anxious again.

"The Finch women might be a lot of things, but mostly we're tenacious," Ruby explained.

"Isn't that the truth." He stifled a laugh. "You know what else is true, though you may find it hard to believe? I'd rather they took everything I owned if it meant Viktor was still alive. I didn't know him long at all, but we had an instant connection that didn't take into account age or experience. He seemed so refreshingly genuine, and I was looking forward to our time together."

Sadness welled up in her and Violet pinched her palm to

keep control. She had a job to do that would hopefully detract from Viktor's senseless death. "Will you be okay staying here by yourself?"

"I guess I'll have to be. I can hardly sell the family home that we've owned for generations, and even if I could, what does that say about me? That I'm a coward and I don't care about other's sacrifices?"

"We wouldn't think that," Ruby told him. "We just want you to be safe."

"That's because you're your mother's daughters."

Ruby smiled tearfully. "Thank you, Arthur, and if you need somewhere to stay until this is sorted, there's always room at our place."

Surprised, Violet glanced at them, but only for a moment. While the invitation sounded so odd, it also felt right.

Arthur swallowed hard. "That is exceptionally kind of you, in light of our history. Let me see what the sheriff says about things, and I'll get back to you, if that's okay?"

"Of course." Ruby smiled and pointed to his desk. "Can I use your computer? I'd like to look something up."

"Help yourself. The password is TullysHotel."

This drew both sister's interest.

Arthur was a little pink-cheeked and he shrugged. "You'll no doubt remember a while back I had plans to develop the town more. I thought a hotel would attract more tourists."

"A hotel would be great, since there's only the resort or the caravan park out of town." Ruby dipped her head and typed in the password while Violet tried to imagine the Arthur of that time dealing in customer service. It would not have been a happy venture for anyone concerned, especially staff.

"Oh, my goodness," Ruby suddenly exclaimed. "It's opened to a password file! I'm not looking Arthur, I promise."

"That's not right." He hurried over and clicked the remaining open tabs. "I always close down my files and laptop when I'm not using them."

Violet carefully put down a Lladro figure, excitement making her fingers shake. "Then if you didn't leave it that way, someone must have been in here who knows the password. That someone is likely the killer and the thief. You better get Nate and tell him what they were looking at." She waited until he was gone. "Nate has been after this person for weeks with no luck. It occurs to me that maybe the person is hiding in plain sight."

"I don't understand the connection." Ruby waved her hand around the room ending at the laptop."

"If they have the house key and can access his accounts and personal files, whoever the killer is, has everything they need to take Arthur's identity."

"Sure, they can do that online, but why do they need his personal possessions?"

"Because they want to be him." Violet nodded as the truth of her words sank in. "That's it. They want everything Arthur has. The question we should ask is whether this is about envy or revenge."

CHAPTER SIXTEEN

The next morning, Nate came through the café door looking like a man on a mission. Luckily he'd just missed the craft group, and the other two customers barely glanced up from their food. Still, he nodded to the kitchen and Violet followed him.

"The autopsy revealed that the bullet that killed Viktor was shot from a very old gun."

Violet frowned. "That was fast. Do you know if it was one of Arthur's guns used?"

He raised an eyebrow as if he hadn't expected her to ask. "That's what we intend to find out. He had a gun safe in the shed. It was locked when I checked, but if the thief had access to a bunch of house keys then maybe the shed key was in with them. I'm going over there soon with tools to break into it because Arthur has no copy."

She snapped her fingers. "Maybe you won't have to. There were pegs for keys on the inside of the pantry."

Again, the eyebrow danced up and down. "How do you know that?"

"I checked inside there the first time he asked me over. I

wasn't being nosey, I just wondered if something might be missing from the room."

Scarlett snorted from where she was loading the oven with small pastries.

Nate's mouth twitched. "From the pantry? I'm not sure what artifacts or possessions Arthur might store in there that would be considered valuable."

She was saved the embarrassment of replying by the front door opening, and hurried out to find that Phin had arrived. He moved to one side as the other customers left.

"You're a day early!"

His ready smile vanished. "Is that a problem?"

Violet grinned. "The exact opposite. We desperately need your expertise."

Nate nodded from beside her. "Hey, Phin. If you wouldn't mind coming with me now, I'd like you to look over the things left behind by a burglar."

"Sure. Though I do need to find a place to stay at some stage. I'd be grateful for any recommendations?"

"You can stay with us." Violet shot a look at Scarlett who nodded. Arthur had stayed the night, but was determined not to be run out of his home. He turned out to be a pleasant if somewhat awkward guest. She wasn't sure Phin would be any better, but it was the right thing to do since he was doing the town a favor.

Phin hesitated. "I don't want to put you out."

"It's no problem at all," Scarlett assured him.

"Now that's settled," Nate headed purposefully toward the door. "Let's get over to Arthur's."

Violet headed him off. "Can I come?"

"Aren't you needed here?" Nate's dryness was becoming a habit.

"Aunt Olivia should be here soon. Do you mind, Scarlett?"

Scarlett waved her away with a resigned expression. "Go, if you must."

Violet didn't need to be told twice, and after grabbing a jacket, followed the men outside.

Phin was about to get into his car when Nate stopped him. "It's just a short walk down the road and there are a few vehicles in the drive that will need to go in and out. You can leave your vehicle here until we get back."

Phin glanced up at the sign which said he had two hours of parking and frowned. "Are you sure it won't take longer?"

"Don't worry about that. You're on police business," Violet chuckled, earning her a disapproving glance from the sheriff, and immediately decided teasing him wasn't in her best interests right now.

The tape remained across Arthur's front door, and this time they went around the back. Deputy Pine was on duty this side of the house, and he touched the rim of his hat as they went by. He seemed pleasant enough when he wasn't stressed out.

"All quiet here, but I haven't seen the mayor, sir."

Nate nodded at the deputy's concern. "I believe Alex took him to see the doctor today for a check-up."

They continued inside via the back door, bypassing the French doors where Viktor's body had lain. No matter that the space was empty, Violet's eyes were still drawn to this area, and she swallowed hard at the memory—and at the stain on the verandah floor.

The conservatory led back into the kitchen and Nate went straight to the pantry, side-stepping the few trinkets that lay nearby.

"There's a light switch just inside on the left," Violet called to him.

The light came on and she heard the jangle of keys. Nate came back out with them and held up an odd looking one.

"Good call, Violet. This looks about right. I'm going to check the gun safe in the shed, why don't you show Phin the pieces of importance first and I'll meet you in the study when I'm done?"

"Okay. Should we wear gloves?"

"Yes. You'll find a pair each on the desk."

Nate looked like a man on a mission and she would have loved to see inside the safe, but Phin was waiting, so she led him to the hall.

"What a mess." Phin gasped. "Looks like the burglar wanted to take everything not nailed down."

"I know what you mean. I'm pretty sure it didn't start out like that."

"What do you mean?"

She told him the story of the botched burglary, the search around town and Ruby's disapearance, and finally Viktor's death.

Phin grimaced and his voice was cool. "You didn't mention murder when you asked me to come."

"It only happened yesterday. I'm sorry, I should have phoned you in case it made you change your mind. I guess I'm so invested in this case now, that it didn't occur to me."

"I see. Obviously the police are looking into the case and have a strong presence in and around the house, but are you sure we're safe here?"

Violet felt terrible. How hadn't she considered this or what his feelings about everything might be? Just because she had to know who was behind all this, it didn't mean everyone else would have the same desire. And, as she said, with the killer still out there, Phin may very well be in danger if he got involved. She swallowed hard. "There's no denying that Viktor was murdered, so I guess we're as safe as we can be until the murderer is caught. Phin, if you aren't comfortable staying, I'm sure the sheriff would be fine for you to leave after you've catalogued this stuff."

He glanced at the items on the floor. "I can't say I'm happy about it, and you know it's a lot more than a couple of hours work here."

"You're right. It was thoughtless of me to bring you here without telling you everything. Do you want to leave now?"

He unexpectedly knelt on the carpet and his breath hissed out. "To be honest I was seriously considering it. Now…not so much."

Her sinking heart lifted at his tone. Was that excitement she heard? Violet leaned over his shoulder. "What have you found?"

He pointed at a pocket watch. "This piece is authentic as far as I can tell without holding it."

Quickly, she snatched the gloves from the desk behind him and handed him a pair. "By giving us the gloves, the sheriff clearly expects us to inspect them thoroughly."

He nodded eagerly and slipped them on. Gingerly he lifted the watch from the floor and cradled it in one hand, then withdrew his loupe from his jacket pocket. "This piece is a German Tambour watch case and dial from the mid-16th century. See the fine engraving on the back."

Side by side their heads almost touching, she let all the information sink in. "Wow! I read up on pocket watches just recently. This movement could fetch an asking price of around £15,000-25,000, which is the approximate US equivalent of $16,500-$28,000, right?"

Phin grinned. "That's exactly right. Well done."

Delighted, Violet waved a hand at the other items nearby. "Do you think all this stuff is authentic?"

"Let's not jump the gun. There is a lot to check and no way of knowing until we do which is or isn't. We need pen and paper." He patted his pockets. "I did bring a pad, but it's in my car."

Violet scrambled to her feet once more and went to the desk. The top was clear except the ink pot and blotter which she didn't like to disturb, so she tried a drawer.

Nate appeared in the doorway. What's all the excitement about?"

"We had a great find and we need some pen and paper, but this drawer is stuck. Any chance you can help get it open?"

He came across the room frowning. "That's odd. I checked out all the drawers last night and they opened fine."

"Maybe you dislodged something."

Nate gave it a firm try, followed by a yank when it didn't budge. The drawer gave way and he almost fell backward. He held it out to her. "There you go."

"Thanks. Yay, there is a pen and notebook in here we can use. And this looks like the thing that jammed it up." She pulled at a piece of paper draped over the back of the drawer which was now torn in one corner.

"What is it?" he asked as she carefully unfolded it.

"A list of some kind. Oh, wait. It's a genealogy report."

"I'll take that." Arthur hurried across the room and snatched the paper from Nate. "This is something I've been working on and nothing to do with the case."

The three of them were surprised at his aggravated manner, and Nate swiftly apologized.

"We weren't snooping," he explained. "Just looking for pen and paper and I didn't think you were home to ask permission. Weren't you seeing the doctor?"

He shoved the paper into his pocket. "That's later this afternoon, and I was resting," he said testily.

"Then, I'm sorry for disturbing you. Phin showed up earlier than expected and I thought it would be a good idea to get started on working out the authenticity of your pieces."

Arthur took a deep breath. "I'm not here to stop you." He shrugged apologetically. "I heard voices and wondered what was going on. I guess I'm a little paranoid these days."

"Understandable given the circumstances. Isn't there somewhere you'd rather be instead of witnessing this all day?" Nate shot Violet a glance.

Arthur noticed and tilted his chin. "It was kind of the girls to give me a bed last night, but as I told you before, I'm not being scared out of my house."

Nate seemed about to argue when Phin stood between them.

"You have some lovely pieces, sir."

"Oh, you two haven't met yet. I apologize." Violet's cheeks heated at overlooking the introductions. No wonder Arthur was upset with a stranger pawing his personal belongings. "Arthur, this is Phin, my assessor friend and mentor. Phin, this is our mayor, Arthur Tully."

Phin removed a glove and they shook hands.

"I'm glad you think so, and I'd be grateful if you can tell me if any of them are genuine, so I can get them insured and put them back where they belong. The house is a mess and...," Arthur's voice wavered. "Well, I'll leave you to it."

Once he left, Violet tutted. "That was awkward and sad—poor Arthur."

Phin sighed. "I've seen a good many people doubting their lives when they lose something important. While it may seem odd to many that possessions could give a person meaning or purpose, for some that's all they have."

Violet nodded slowly. "I would never have looked at it like that before we sold Mom's book. The book itself meant nothing apart from it belonging to her. That was the key."

"We all like to know where we came from."

Phin's words hung over her like the smoke from Absolum's cigarette in Alice in Wonderland. It must be Arthur's genealogy list that was bringing back all the memories of the Finch girls' own heirloom. With not much else left to them except the run-down house, the book they found opened the past in ways they would never forget. Selling it gave them the promise of a better life, but they hadn't done it lightly. In a way, it was finding out the story behind it that made it possible to let the book go. Maybe that's all Arthur wanted—to know what his things meant to those who came before him.

Which meant they needed to see that list. By checking on a select item's history, they might find out who brought the treasures into this house, and when. This could show them who might have a motive, and finding the killer would surely bring Arthur the peace of mind he needed. It would also assist with the valuations to get the right insurance cover.

The problem was, judging by the way Arthur had clasped it to his chest, she didn't fancy her chances of getting it off him. Why was that?

Violet also had to wonder why he didn't already have any of his possessions insured.

CHAPTER SEVENTEEN

Perched on the spare comfy chair, Violet noted down the names of each piece before Phin checked them over from Arthur's desk chair beside her. He called out numbers, dates, and the names of stamps if they had any. Thanks to her recent studies, she managed to recall some facts on several items and made her own assessments in a separate column.

Phin devised the system for her to make the most of this opportunity to learn the trade as they worked and despite how this all came about, a thrill went through her with each correct assessment, though she couldn't deny a pang of guilt at enjoying it so much.

Though the bulk of Arthur's treasures came from the 20th century, she was sure there were pieces from the watch's era as well as the 18th and 19th century. He clearly valued them, regardless of their worth, and even though not everything was worth more than sentimental value, these were Arthur's personal possessions, and they took care with each item.

After nearly two hours of intense scrutiny, Phin rubbed his eyes. He stood and stretched, his back cracking. "Any chance of coffee?"

Violet blinked in surprise. "I just realized you've had nothing since you arrived. I'm embarrassed for being such a terrible host."

He laughed her concern away. "I'm fine, just in need of a recharge."

"No, you aren't fine, and coffee isn't enough to sustain anybody," Violet insisted. "Let's go back to the café and get you some lunch—and as much coffee as you can drink."

"Perfect, I can move my car while I'm there."

She grinned. "I'm sure it's still there."

He tutted at her teasing and dragged on his coat. The thought of being late to move his car clearly still bugged him and she chuckled. He and Scarlett were both sticklers for the right way to do things. Although, when it came to their professions, that was probably better than Violet's way, which was a sobering thought.

Nate stood outside having a meeting with his three deputies. As soon as he saw them he hurried over to the veranda. "Anything wrong?"

"For a change, no," Violet assured him. "We're off to the café. Do you want anything? I can bring something back."

He tilted his head as if it were a hard decision. "That's okay. I was about to have a break myself, so I might join you."

Maybe the break was true, but she thought it more likely that the sheriff was happy to have an excuse to see Scarlett again. "Sure. Did you find out if the gun was Arthur's?"

"You never forget anything, do you?" He gave her a side-eye.

She grinned, taking it as a compliment. If she was going to be an assessor, Violet had to learn a lot of facts and dates and have them stay close to the surface in her mind, or at least reachable. It was a challenge and one she relished, so remembering the keys and what Nate was primarily here for had been no-brainers.

Nate appeared to be considering if he would tell her. Eventually, he sighed. "As it turns out, yes, it is. And the safe hadn't been tampered with, so it wasn't broken into."

"It's odd that the keys were still hanging in the pantry. In fact, when you think how many times this person has been inside the house without breaking in, and the ability to get into the safe, you have to wonder what their main purpose is when they could have taken everything and been long gone by now."

"You don't have to wonder about any of it," he said pointedly.

"That's easy to say. If a person can get in and out of Arthur's place on a whim, what's to stop them robbing the rest of the town?"

Phin put his hand up. "Sorry to interrupt Violet, but I imagine that the criminal has another set of keys to this house, but not anywhere else. Otherwise, the sheriff would have heard about it by now."

Violet pumped a fist in the air. "Of course, there must be another set of keys other than the ones in the pantry,and Arthur must know who would have access to them."

"I think you missed the point that Phin was making about other houses being safe." Nate shook his head at her. "Anyway, I've already asked Arthur and he only knows of three sets which are accounted for."

"If that is true and the thief can get in any time they like—day or night—without disturbing anyone that must mean that someone cut a new set." She raised an eyebrow. "Unless you have another theory."

He made a grumbling noise and ushered them down the street to the café where he held the door open for her. "I'll have coffee hot and strong, please."

Olivia was at the counter, and she shared a smile with Violet when Nate tried to peer around them into the kitchen as though he were looking for something—or someone.

"Let me get that for you sheriff." Olivia picked up the coffee pot. "It's so nice to see you again, Phin. What about you?"

Phin tipped his hat. "You're looking lovely as ever Ms. Greene, and I'll have the same thank you."

Olivia flushed a little, not good with taking a compliment or a touch of flirting—just like Violet and her sisters. "Would you like a bite to eat? Scarlett makes a lovely chicken and cranberry panini."

"That sounds delicious."

Scarlett arrived, wiping her hands on her apron, and smiling at both men. "How is it going at Arthur's?"

"Slowly, I'm afraid." Despite his comment, Nate smiled back.

While the dewy-eyed looks made Violet pleased that her plans to get these two together were playing out as she intended, she was anxious to get to the bottom of Arthur's dilemma and couldn't help being more excited about that. "We think we have the solution to how the thief is getting in and out—once we figure out who has access to Arthur's spare keys."

Nate glanced around the café which was empty. "Just because you are privy to information about the case doesn't mean you should state things about it to the world," he warned.

"Sorry, but I didn't think it would hurt when it's only us here." She swept an arm around the room, and it occurred to her that it was unusually quiet. "Hmmm. Where is everyone?"

Scarlett blew a raspberry. "Don't think that it's been like this the whole time. You just missed the craft group, and the lunch rush is over."

Violet looked at her watch. "Good grief. The day has flown."

"I guess everyone is busy," Scarlett said. "How is Arthur today?"

"He seems to be okay. He's having his check up with the doctor and Alex insisted on taking him," Nate explained.

Olivia nodded approvingly. "Alex is proving to be an asset to the community in many ways."

"I am worried about him though. Because he got him the job, he feels responsible for Viktor and somehow ensuring Arthur stays safe makes him feel like he's doing something to atone for his death. Or at least have it not be in vain." Violet sighed. "He takes things very personally and losing Viktor has upset him more than he'll ever show."

Scarlett chewed her lip. "I get that impression too. Luckily, he has Ruby to help him with his grief."

"And his sister." Nate frowned. "Speaking of which, has anyone seen Lexie lately?"

Scarlett gasped. "You're surely not suggesting Lexie has anything to do with this? She barely knows Arthur and that poor girl has been through enough."

Violet studied her sister, who apparently bore no grudge against Lexie. When that poor little rich girl's fiancé had been murdered by one of Lexie's father's cohorts a while back, it came to light that Scarlett's boyfriend, Sam, the local paramedic, and Lexie were in love. Violet wasn't so sure she'd be as understanding and judging by Nate's interested look, he couldn't quite believe it either.

"I'm only asking after her, because I haven't seen her around and with Alex being so upset at the loss of his friend I imagine she would want to be there for him as he was for her," Nate stated. "Wouldn't you agree?"

Scarlett tipped her chin. "Perhaps she's out of town with her boyfriend."

The last thing anyone needed was for these two to get into a test over whether Scarlett was in fact truly over Sam. Violet pushed by them and began making lattes for herself and Scarlett knowing her sister forgot to take a break more often than not. "Any chance of feeding us something substantial so we can get back to the collating?"

Olivia tutted loudly. "You can't be expected to work productively with no fuel. Isn't that what your mom always said, girls? I'll toast those paninis and bring out some hot soup as well."

"Let me give you a hand, Ms. Greene." Phin followed her before anyone could stop him.

"Now, that is cute." Violet chuckled and handed Nate a mug.

He looked at her blankly and from behind him Scarlett grinned. Men couldn't always see the obvious.

Not even clued-up sheriffs.

CHAPTER EIGHTEEN

After lunch they continued the cataloging back at Arthur's and by the end of the day had covered a good deal of Arthur's possessions. Violet and Phin were taking a well-earned break in the kitchen when Arthur returned from his appointment and joined them, sitting glumly at the table. Alex came in soon after with the weary looking sheriff. It had been a long day for them all, and though Arthur told them the doctor was happy with the check-up, Violet thought all the men needed cheering up.

She placed a fresh pot of tea, Arthur's favorite, in front of him. "Phin and I have found that some of your items have wonderful history and could be worth quite a bit. One in particular."

He scowled. "If I wanted to sell them—which I don't."

Mortified that he thought this, she stammered. "No, I…I wasn't suggesting that."

"I think what Violet means is that the more expensive items could have been the incentive for your thief," Phin explained in his quiet and sensitive manner.

"Then why are the majority of them still here?" This time Arthur's voice was more plaintive than accusatory.

"Because the person killed Viktor," Alex grunted. "And they don't want to be found with the stolen goods."

Violet poured tea for the men. "I mostly agree with Alex, only it feels like a jigsaw that we haven't pieced together quite right, and we're still missing the crucial piece."

"Like what?" Arthur pulled his cup toward him and sipped appreciatively.

"That's the million-dollar question," Nate said before gratefully accepting the cup of coffee he preferred from Violet.

She had been pondering this over the last few hours. "Did you get in touch with the housekeeper yet about her set of keys?"

"I did. Mrs. Harris insisted she'd handed back her keys on her last day of work."

"I told you she had," Arthur insisted. "They're the ones in the pantry."

"You know what I think?"

Nate raised an eyebrow at her. "Is there a way to stop you from telling us?"

She shrugged the sarcasm off. "Those keys were the first reason to break in."

"That's just it, there was no break-in," Nate reminded her.

"Not as such, but bear with me a second. Arthur, like the rest of Cozy Hollow, dosen't always lock up, right?"

Everyone stared at her blankly, so she continued.

"Unlike the rest of us, Arthur probably has more items that are worth stealing. I'm thinking that the thief was making a lengthy plan to take a few pieces at a time, and they wanted access day or night. They took the keys that Arthur never uses, copied them, and put them back, avoiding any suspicion in case their disappearance would have been noted down the track." She sat back and crossed her arms. "Now they have a set of keys to every door on the property, including the gun cabinet."

Phin steepled his fingers together under his chin. "That makes sense to me. Also, and it is only an opinion, which I hope you won't mind me giving, listening to you all discuss the case over the course of the day makes me think this person didn't have murder on their mind."

"That's right," Violet agreed. "It seems like, as time went by, they got more vindictive. They wanted Arthur's stuff, and they also wanted to scare him."

Arthur grimaced. "And make me think I'm losing my mind."

Violet paced the kitchen. "Hmmm. This person knows you very well. They know about you and your family history." She looked around at the group who were possibly in the line of fire by being involved. Those who didn't know all the facts, should be informed sooner rather than later. "And they know about the troubles you had a while back."

Arthur shifted in his chair. "They could have got all that from the papers, or asking around."

"Sure, but one of us would have heard about a stranger asking questions."

That stilled the room for a few minutes, giving Violet the space to ask a tasteless question. "Arthur, do you have a will?"

He shrugged. "Everyone should, and before you get excited, mine is very cut and dried."

"You might think so." She saw Nate about to interfere and blurted. "Are you leaving anything to perhaps an estranged family member or an ex-employee?"

Arthur once again shifted uncomfortably. "No."

Nate sat forward. "Arthur, I should have asked you about this earlier. It was remiss of me because I'd always understood that you had no family. Which is absolutely no excuse. Who stands to benefit if something happens to you?"

Arthur grunted. "It's no one's business what I do with my estate."

"Normally I'd agree, but this situation is anything but normal. After everything that's happened, and now the murder of Viktor, perhaps how they get hold of your wealth is no longer important to the killer. I've seen it before, once a criminal crosses the line, even accidentally, things can escalate."

"Accidently?" Alex growled. "Didn't you notice that Viktor was clearly shot in the back by this coward!"

Arthur paled. "All right, I concede that in the unlikely event that someone got hold of my will, which I can assure you is in my safe, they might want to hurry things along, but I'll only tell you the beneficiary in private, Sheriff."

Disappointment almost choked Violet. She truly felt that they were on the edge of unraveling this mystery and that Arthur unwittingly held that missing piece she'd spoken of. Why was it such a secret who he was leaving everything to?

Alex scraped back his chair and stomped to the door. "I'm going to check the grounds again."

"He's angry with me." Arthur said sadly after the door closed rather firmly behind him.

Violet patted his shoulder. "Don't take it personally. He's terribly upset to lose his closest friend, and frustrated that the killer hasn't been caught yet."

"Does he think I don't want that?"

"Naturally, he wants justice for Viktor, and I'm sure it seems to him and others," Nate glanced pointedly at Violet, "that we're not doing enough."

"I'm sure you're doing everything you can." She regretted her ability to put her foot in her mouth at any opportunity, but still had the need to explain. "Only, for those of us not working in your field it does feel like it takes an awful long time."

"Whatever you think of the wheels of justice moving slowly," Nate said a touch caustically, "I have to do things by the book, and yes, that can slow the process down, but it is a process."

"I'm sure everyone is doing what they can," Phin interjected tactfully.

Arthur sighed heavily. "We should allow the sheriff to do his job. My trinkets are of no concern when we're talking about people's lives."

"But..."

"Please, Violet. I've had enough."

Enough? Violet wasn't sure what Arthur meant exactly. They'd all had enough of secrets and death, but the person responsible had to be found and she just knew that something in Arthur's possessions was at the center of this.

Phin stood. "We'll leave you in peace, Arthur, and come back tomorrow morning with the final analysis of our findings."

"Then you'll be done?" Arthur asked hopefully.

"Yes, and I'm sorry that it's dragged on," Violet said sympathetically. "You must feel like your house is not your own."

"That's true, but I am grateful for your help."

Violet smiled and led Phin outside. "If only he didn't sound like he was merely being polite," she told him quietly. "I worry that he's getting sick again."

"Wait up, the sheriff wants me to walk you back," Deputy Pine called from behind them. He caught up, taking notice of everything around them.

Crazily, Violet hadn't thought about their safety and was grateful that Nate had. They walked in silence to the café where Scarlett was in the process of closing for the day. She looked exhausted and again that guilt struck Violet squarely between the shoulders.

"Thank you for the escort, Deputy Pine."

"You're welcome ma'am. It's just a shame we can't do this for everybody."

An unexpected starkness caught her off guard. Violet supposed this was preferential treatment, but then again, they were helping the case—hopefully. "Yes, I'm sure people feel unable to walk about as freely. I don't think we've been properly introduced. What is your name?"

"Christopher. Everyone calls me Chris." He straightened perceptibly. "When I'm out of uniform, that is."

"Of course. And I'm Violet. This is Phineas and my sister Scarlett. See you tomorrow, perhaps."

"Yes, ma'am. Have a good night." He touched the brim of his hat to each of them, the way Nate did and hurried back to Arthur's.

"He seems nice," she told Scarlett and Phin.

"That's the first time he's been in here," Scarlett noted. "I think he's been thrown in the deep end since he arrived, which must be tough, because he's probably had no time to make friends."

"Well, he seems to be coping very well and from what I've witnessed, takes his position seriously. Anyway, I'm starving. Do you want me to whip up some pasta when we get home?"

Scarlett sighed. "Any other day, I'd say yes, but as there's been a serious decline in the customers who come in on their own, we have so much left-over stock. I think we should use some of it at least. Do you mind, Phin?"

"Not at all. It would be such a shame to waste any of your wonderful baking."

That made her sister smile and Violet was both relieved and dismayed. She felt as exhausted as Scarlett looked, so not cooking was a relief, but how long could the café, and the town in general, cope with the lack of business? Not to mention the lack of freedom. Violet's determination to find this person would undoubtedly keep her awake tonight and it didn't make her feel any better that so many others would be experiencing the same worries and desperation.

They packed up a selection of food and headed home where Ruby was collecting eggs out the back, with George and Bob at her heels.

"Hi, Phin. I'm so glad to see you all safe at home. Cozy Hollow is like a ghost town and without any customers, I kept the library doors locked for most of the day."

"How did you get on with Arthur's family history?" Violet asked.

"Nothing out of the ordinary, but I found photos of Arthur wearing his watch."

Scarlett pushed between them. "Okay, no talk of Arthur's things or the killer at least until after dinner. Which will be ready in half an hour."

"Fine," Violet agreed, though she had a ton of questions. "Phin, I'll show you to your room if it's ready."

"I changed the bedding when I got home," Ruby assured her.

"Great. Once Phin is settled, I'll feed the pets and set the table."

This was the way it was in the Finch household. No shirkers and a sense of routine kept them living together mostly harmoniously. That and lack of funds. While sometimes they would all like their own space, this worked just fine for the foreseeable future. Of course, that might change when one of them got serious about a partner.

Violet wondered if it would be Ruby or Scarlett?

CHAPTER NINETEEN

By an agreement made the night before, Phin came into town with Ruby, so he didn't have to get up when Scarlett and Violet did to get to the café. All the bread was made, albeit a reduced amount, and was in the display case by the time he arrived.

Having eaten his breakfast with Ruby, Phin insisted on clearing tables while the sisters had a break. After that they were ready to head over to Arthur's, but before she could step outside, Phin took Violet's arm.

"I worked on the file last night and feel confident that we've checked every item in enough detail. Now it's simply a matter of giving Arthur a letter of authentication for each one. I can do that when I get back to my office and FedEx them to him."

"Are you saying that you don't need me there today?"

"It's more that there isn't anything else for you to do." He explained. "I'm sure you have more important work to do here. I'll send you through what I would say to a client and how I would present my findings."

Disappointed, Violet would have loved to be there and

witness that side of the proceedings, but Phin was right, she was needed here. Scarlett's face told her how much she needed another pair of hands. Business was picking up and it was too much for one person.

After all that had happened, it seemed that life had suddenly returned to normal. Yes, there was a thief and a murderer still out there, but maybe they had moved on, which might be better for Cozy Hollow as a whole.

At lunchtime Ruby dropped in to see if Scarlett was okay, not knowing that Violet was there. Suddenly, Olivia burst through the door, her hair shockingly awry as if she'd been tugging on it. "Something awful has happened!"

"I don't know if I can handle anything else," Violet muttered before easing Olivia into the closest chair since she appeared to be on the verge of collapsing.

"I can hear you very well, thank you, Violet, and it's not like I wanted it to end like this."

Their aunt wasn't prone to sniping, proving she was definitely out of sorts, and Ruby thrust a coffee mug into Olivia's shaking hands. "Whatever it is sounds serious."

"It's all turned to custard, and I don't know what I'm going to do," Olivia all but wailed.

Used to Olivia's outbursts, Scarlett continued to glaze fruit pies. "I'm sorry you're upset Olivia, but you'll have to give us a clue."

Olivia pursed her lips. "I'm talking about selling my shop —it's not happening now."

There was a collective gasp from the sisters and one pie got more than its fair share of glaze before Violet wrested the jug from her sister's hands.

However, Ruby was the quickest to recover. "Oh dear. That isn't good. Do your friends not want it anymore?"

Their aunt bent her head and sniffed into a crumpled tissue. "They had a terrible fight about who will own the most, and therefore get to make decisions. Things got a little testy, which isn't unusual with that lot. Before I saw it coming, words boiled over. I did my best to talk them around, but they couldn't agree on anything after that, and now they're walking away from the agreement."

The sisters hid grins because they could picture the dust up of the feisty group. However, it really wasn't funny. Without the sale, Olivia couldn't work in the café, and without another employee, Violet couldn't pursue her career. That sobered her up in a flash and she could see by Scarlett's wide eyes that it had just occurred to her too.

Ruby knelt at Olivia's side. "Maybe if I go talk to them and see if there's a way to make them appreciate that one argument doesn't have to change their plans."

"Would you, dear?" Olivia's eyes lit with hope. "If anyone could make them see sense, it's you. Only, they are so mad with each other, I don't know how you'll get them to listen."

"None of them have been in today and it's already lunchtime," Scarlett noted.

"The fight only happened this morning." Olivia sniffed again. "I was in the shop showing them how to work the register for the tenth time. I swear I was being patient, but they didn't like being told what to do and kept getting it wrong. Some people are so stubborn! I don't know why I'm still friends with them."

Ruby hugged her. "Because you have been since you were children, and one little spat won't change that."

Violet wasn't so sure. While she had faith in Ruby's abilities to charm most people, what if the argument was about more than wanting to be the top dog. Cold feet could happen in business just like relationships, couldn't it?

"Perhaps they've decided that running the shop is too much for them." She shouldn't have said it and when Olivia's face fell even further, wished she hadn't. It was the very reason Olivia wanted to sell. Even with many years of experience, ultimately it was now proving a lot for one person. She couldn't remember any of her aunt's group of friends working full-time, and once they investigated it properly, so many aspects about running their own business would no doubt seem an insurmountable challenge.

Scarlett grimaced and turned to Ruby. "Doesn't Mrs. Night come to the library every afternoon?"

"Oh, shoot. I better get back there to let her in. Thanks for lunch, Scarlett."

"Ruby?" Violet called.

Her sister whirled at the door. "Mmmm?"

"Now that the lunch rush is dying down, would you mind if I tagged along?"

"Do you need a book?"

Sometimes Violet wondered about Ruby's super intelligence. "Not today, Rubes. I thought it might be a good opportunity to talk to Mrs. Night about the craft shop—without her friends around."

"Duh." Ruby tapped the side of her head. "What a good idea. Then we can get to the bottom of why they've changed their minds, and think of a way to change them back."

Olivia's eyes twinkled. "Violet, you're a natural at this sleuthing stuff. Linda is certainly the one more likely to spill the beans on the real reason."

"Don't forget to let us know how you get on," Scarlett saw them to the door. "I'm counting on you two to get this sorted, otherwise life is going to get very tricky around here."

All three of them grimaced. It was nothing compared to what Arthur was going through, but it would absolutely affect them all.

CHAPTER TWENTY

Linda Night was waiting at the library door peering through the window at the side and twisting the ornate door knob back and forth. She swung around when she heard them coming.

"Goodness, I was worried that you were kidnapped, Ruby. I was just about to go ask Scarlett if you were okay, but it took a lot to walk here from my place even though it's just around the corner, and I was getting more anxious by the minute. If only I hadn't read everything in the house."

"Sorry to keep you waiting, Mrs. Night. Scarlett made a lunch too delicious to ignore, and the library has been so quiet the last couple of days."

The more easy-going of the craft group chuckled. "Well, now, I can understand the call of your sister's baking. Sometimes I don't cook all week because I can't resist buying her food."

She followed Ruby inside with Violet trailing after them.

"I'm sure Scarlett appreciates your business. Aside from the anxiety, how are you, Mrs. Night?" Ruby enquired sweetly.

Her mouth turned down a little. "To tell the truth, I've been better. What with all this drama around the mayor and that poor man being killed, I was almost put off my food. Then there was the terrible..." She stopped and glanced around wildly.

"It's okay, Mrs. Kight. There's no one else here and Violet and I already heard about the fight."

Her eyes widened. "Did you? Goodness, there are no secrets in Cozy Hollow, are there? You do understand that it wasn't my fault things aren't going ahead with buying the craft store. I had my husband's will money earmarked for the new adventure and was raring to go. But those other two were at each other like a couple of witches at Halloween. I told them there was surely a solution, but they dug their toes and fingers in so deep, I couldn't shift them." Her mouth turned down.

"I'm sure you did your best to talk them around. I suppose, Ms. Wolf put in the lion's share, so she wanted to be in charge?"

"Oh, you are clever." Linda glanced around again and lowered her voice. "Leona has very specific ideas and poo-pooed anything Gail and I suggested. And worse, I could see Olivia didn't like what Leona intended to do to the store."

Violet winced, wondering if their aunt had caused the breakdown after all. "It must have been one heck of a change, if Aunt Olivia objected."

Linda chewed her bottom lip for a moment. "To be honest, she didn't say a word. However, I did think she was going to be violently ill when Leona said that the spinning wheel would have to go and that she would hang her latest quilt in the window instead."

Horrified at the iconic wheel missing from main street, Violet couldn't fathom a reason for removing it from the large window. "Is the quilt good enough to replace it?"

"Violet!" Ruby warned.

"What? I'm just asking why Olivia would object if it was such a masterpiece."

Linda snorted. "Unfortunately, Violet is on the right track, too." She lowered her voice further, despite them being the only ones in the library. "It's quite hideous, but who would be brave enough to say so? Not me, that's for sure."

Vindicated, Violet continued. "So, if no one mentioned the issues with the offending quilt, the fight began over something else, right?"

"It sure did." Linda leaned forward and theatrically paused for a second while the tension built. "It was the worse suggestion ever! She wants to change the name of the store."

Violet blinked hard. "What? From Cozy Crafts?"

Linda quivered from head to toe. "I know it's a shocking idea, isn't it? And not in keeping with the town theme at all. Arthur would have had a fit if he got wind of it and the committee? Well, it would be an all out war!"

Since all the shops' names had the word 'Cozy' in the title it also seemed counter-productive for a new business. "By bringing up something so controversial, do you think Mrs. Wolf was looking for a way out?"

"I don't understand why you'd ask that, Violet." Linda sniffed. "The three of us have talked about nothing else for months. We all had so many plans and our own ideas. Now none of them will come to pass because none of us can afford a venture like owning a store on our own."

Violet hadn't intended to upset her, and she had a great deal of empathy. After all, spreading the workload was the very reason she still worked in the café and why Ruby still helped there when she could. The sinking feeling that she would be stuck in the café for the rest of her life hit her once more and she shook herself like Bob did when he wanted to reset his thinking.

Somehow she had to talk Leona around and she couldn't do that unless she found out the real reason for the fight. It was incredibly important to sort it out soon, but was it as important as catching a killer?

"I won't make any promises, Mrs. Night, but we'll have a chat with Mrs. Wolf and get to the bottom of it," Ruby told her gently.

"I'd be so grateful if you could sort it out and so would Gail."

Violet coughed. "We will do our best. Perhaps you could help us with something else?"

Linda's eyes lit up. "Anything, dear."

"The woman who worked for Arthur. What was she like?"

"Imogen is lovely. I admit that Leona was right about her not being the best cook, but she did try and she keeps a clean and tidy house. In fact, she's a little persnickety when it comes to housework, liking things just so. I'm sure that's what appealed to Arthur." She leaned into the sisters. "Just between us, though I really shouldn't gossip—I think she did have her sights set on him and when it didn't go the way she hoped, too much work was the best excuse. We all know Arthur has only ever loved one woman, so a replacement would have to be more than that."

Linda fluffed her bottle-blonde hair and Violet wondered if she fancied herself as that replacement. Everyone in town had been well aware of Arthur's infatuation for their mom. He hadn't been able to hide his feelings, so there was no point in denying it, but she'd be darned if she would discuss it.

"Did she have another job to go to?"

Linda's forehead furrowed. "Sorry?"

"Imogen—After leaving Arthur's employment, is she working somewhere else now?"

"No. It was a hasty decision and her son wasn't happy that she'd thrown away a perfectly good job."

"How do you know about that?"

"She's a friend of mine," Linda stated matter-of-factly.

Violet gaped. "I didn't know."

Linda chuckled. "I daresay, I don't know all your friends either."

"Where does she live? And what kind of car does she drive?"

"About five miles out of town. I'm not sure why you need to know, but she doesn't have a car so her son always brought her to work. Unfortunately, they had a huge argument and he's moved out of home. Not before time, in my opinion."

Violet smiled encouragingly. "I'm interested to know if she saw any strange people around the mayor's house while she worked there."

"She's a very private person and took her job seriously. I'm sure the sheriff would have spoken to her about that, but she certainly didn't mention to me anything about strangers."

"I'm sure you're right about the sheriff and your friend sounds lovely, Mrs. Night. I'm not sure if we've ever met. Would she have been in the café anytime?"

"I shouldn't think so. After her husband died she's struggled to make ends meet, and rarely treats herself." Linda flushed. "Oh dear, I shouldn't gossip about her, but it is widely known in our age group."

Ruby gave a sharp cough. "Violet, don't you think you should get back to the mayor's place? I'm sure the sheriff wants to finish up there today."

She blinked at her sister who was waggling her eyebrows and nodding at the door. Obviously Ruby thought she could get more information from Gail using a more convivial approach. "You're right. I'll pick up that book later," she added in case there was any question as to why she was there in the first place.

After a quick goodbye she ran as fast as she could to Arthur's. She wasn't exactly scared, she told herself. It was more of a precaution .

A shadow stepped out of the line of trees and her heart threatened to leap from her chest.

CHAPTER TWENTY-ONE

A scream died in her throat. "Alex! Could you stop doing that."

He merely raised an eyebrow. "I heard running and wanted to make sure you weren't someone that isn't welcome, and meant Arthur harm. The element of surprise helps convince people to rethink their plans—among other things."

In his last job he was head of security at the wood carver's warehouses in Harmony Beach and she shivered at the prospect of what else heading off a would-be assassin or thief might entail. Whatever it was, he was undeniably calm about the prospect. She swallowed hard. "I need to see the sheriff immediately."

"He's in the kitchen with Arthur and a locksmith. I'm sure he'll be happy to see you."

That's when she noticed a van at the end of the driveway just past the house. It sported a sign across the back doors saying Keith's Cozy Keys. "Thanks." Violet ignored what could be a touch of sarcasm over the sheriff's delight at her arrival, and carried on around the back.

The men sat at the kitchen table where the locksmith was writing a list of locks to change.

"Sorry to barge in," she called from the small veranda.

Arthur stood and offered her his chair. "You're very flushed, dear. Are you all right?"

"I'm fine, thank you. I've come from the library."

"Reading is good." The locksmith nodded. "Pity more don't do it instead of terrorizing the neighborhood for a hobby."

Violet didn't offer the insight that killing a person might not be considered a hobby. Besides, who could truly say with any conviction right now why this was happening? "While I agree, I wasn't there to read." She gave the sheriff a pointed look.

Nate narrowed his gaze. "How about you get started Keith, while Arthur and I have a word with Violet."

"Good idea. I'll do the front and back door, then the gun safe which will take the longest. If you think of any more I might need to do, I can come back and change them tomorrow."

Arthur nodded. "Thanks, Keith."

"Let's go into the office," Nate suggested and led the way.

Violet shut the door after them. "I don't know how much digging you did on Imogen Harris, and please don't let her know I told you this, but Linda Night says she left not just because of the work and that she desperately needed the money."

Arthur put up a hand. "You can stop right there, dear. Imogen and I go way back. She's a good woman and I put too much on her and paid her too little for it. I regret that and the way we parted."

"You told me it was a mutual split," Nate countered.

"Well, I guess that's how I wanted it to be." The tips of his ears looked ready to burst into flames.

So, Arthur hadn't been truthful, and Violet wondered if this wasn't the only thing he was keeping from them. "Did you two have a relationship at any stage?" She expected Nate to intervene, but instead he watched Arthur intently.

"No." Arthur stiffened, but Nate's stare seemed to wear him down quickly. "We were friendly at school, but she got married as soon as we left."

Violet didn't believe him. Those ear tips didn't lie, and it could be said that the mayor had embellished the truth when it suited him in the past. She made her voice as gentle as possible. "According to Linda, Imogen had a torch for you since way back."

He gave a half-hearted laugh. "You don't want to pay too much heed to Linda Night. She's known for her light touch on the truth and heavy hand on gossip. Now, was that all?"

"Just one more thing." She pointed across the room. "Your safe, will you change the combination?"

"I already have."

"And you've told no one the new combination?"

"Certainly not," he huffed indignantly and stalked out of the room.

Violet knew then he really was hiding something, and she'd bet a batch of berry muffins that it was to do with Imogen and an infatuation that perhaps wasn't as one-sided as he wanted them to believe. She turned to Nate. "I'd like to meet Imogen."

Narrow-eyed he growled. "Could I see your contract?"

"What contract?"

"You seem to be under the illusion that you've been hired to conduct this investigation."

"No, I'm not," she said defensively. "It's just that I think Arthur isn't being entirely truthful. If that's the case, you'll never solve the crime because he's probably protecting the one person who may have the facts we're missing."

Arms crossed he leaned toward her. "Me and my department are missing them. Not you or us."

Deflated, she shrugged. "Fine. Imogen is the key here and if you're allowing her to walk away with information that might catch the killer, I guess you have your reasons."

"I'm not doing any such thing and I don't know how you came to that conclusion. I have spoken to her and considering what you've said, I'll talk to her again. You on the other hand need to finish up here, so Phin can go home."

"Yes, Sir," she snipped. "Where is he by the way?"

"He's around somewhere chatting with my deputies. I've asked him not to, but he said they fascinate him. Yet another reminder that my badge counts for very little," he said through gritted teeth.

She knew she antagonized him. All the Finch women did. But he was even more tetchy this morning. As he marched off, she appreciated that her mood was equally dark. How could she blame him for feeling out of control when there was so much going on here that none of them understood?

Just because they had been through so much with Nate, didn't give her any rights. That was a fact and she understood it. Only, she had such a strong conviction about Imogen Harris holding the answers, it was going to be almost impossible to sit on her hands and do nothing.

Who was she kidding? 'Almost' didn't factor into it. She was going to find out all she could about Imogen. Maybe Scarlett could sweet talk Nate into giving up any information he had as well. Although, that might be too much to ask for right now since the couple seemed to be at loggerheads—again. Plus, Nate would assume that Scarlett would pass along anything he told her.

She strode out of the house and found Phin talking to Deputy Pine.

"So you're new to this?" Phin asked.

"Fresh out of college, sir."

"The sheriff tells me you were top of your class."

"Yes, sir," he said proudly. "Before I joined, I was thinking about signing up for the army because I'm a crack shot, but the idea of going to war upset my mom. She's on her own on a small farm the other side of Destiny and couldn't manage if I got myself killed."

"That was very responsible of you, son."

Just then her phone buzzed in her pocket. It was a message from Ruby.

"Can you come back to the library. It won't take long?"

Violet felt the pull, as if she already knew this was going to be a breakthrough. This feeling happened often enough to trust it. "Ruby needs me at the library. I won't be long."

"No need to hurry," Phin told her.

The deputy tipped his hat at Phin then turned to her. "I've been instructed to go with you, Ms. Finch."

"Really? When did Nate say that?"

Disgruntled, he waved her forward. "The sheriff gave me the instructions as ongoing until the case is solved."

"For me or everyone?"

"For whoever he tells me to escort at the time." He dismissed her argument.

She was used to being put in her place for daring to quibble, but the situation didn't sit right with her. While she was happy to have the escort, it seemed unlikely that many people were being afforded the same courtesy. Which was troubling, when clearly the Finch women were considered more at risk.

"Please let the sheriff know where I've gone." Deputy Pine told Phin over his shoulder.

Then they were on their way. A person could get dizzy

with all the back and forth, but Violet knew Ruby wouldn't call her to the library for nothing. It seemed like the old building held many secrets just waiting to be uncovered and Ruby had a talent for hunting them out.

CHAPTER TWENTY-TWO

Violet had to knock on the library door, since they had all decided this was the best precaution.

Ruby let her in, her eyes dancing and led her to one of the reading desks where she laid a book gently in front of Violet. "You need to take a look at this."

"I don't have time to go through year books."

"I suggest you make time." Ruby tapped the page, pointing to a young woman who was so much like Ruby it made Violet's heart ache. "See this picture? Notice anything familiar."

Irrationally, Violet's stomach sank a little. Ruby looked okay, but there was always a nagging fear that one of her sisters would get sick with cancer like their mom had. "I can see it's Mom, but why are you looking at this now? Is something wrong with you? Tell me it's only because you miss her."

Ruby gave a small smile. "I always do, and I'm fine. Look closer at the rest of the page, Vi."

With a sigh of relief, she did as instructed. It was their parent's year book from Cozy Hollow High School. As it was a small town, the class wasn't huge. She thought she recognized a few faces, but what did they have to do with finding a killer? Then her focus zoned in on one person more than the others.

"Wait, is that Arthur?" A younger version of the mayor stood behind Lilac Finch. His gaze was not directed at the camera. Instead, he wore a dreamy expression fixed on the girl in front of him.

"It sure is. Doesn't he look cute?" Ruby's mouth twitched.

Violet nodded. Not a particularly tall man, Arthur looked fit and healthy with a great deal of wavy fair hair. "Who would have thought?"

"And check out this person right here…"

The excitement in her sister's voice grew, and Violet checked out the attractive brunette then ran her finger along the names printed below the picture and read aloud. "Imogen Carrington. Oh. It's Imogen Harris!"

"That's right. And next to Arthur is her husband to be."

The way Arthur looked at their mom was mirrored by how Jim Harris was looking at Imogen. "You're right, this is interesting. It makes sense that they all went to school together and were the same age, so they probably hung out a lot, but I still don't get the importance of it today."

"Turn the page," Ruby demanded, hopping from one foot to the other.

Dutifully she did and found another picture of the class together. This one was far more candid, and it was clear that there were others who might be considered couples. It was also clear by the way she was looking at Arthur that Imogen wasn't as interested in Jim as he was in her.

"Hah. So, Arthur was in love with mom, who was in love with dad, while Imogen was in love with Arthur who didn't know she was alive."

"That might be a little strong on Imogen's behalf, but I think it might be pretty darn close to the truth."

Violet reluctantly let the book be pushed away and Ruby placed a document in the space. "It's a birth certificate," she noted.

"That's right. For a Jeffrey Harris. If you look at the date, he's a couple of years older than Scarlett."

Violet read it and shrugged. "Am I missing something?"

Almost gleefully, Ruby spread a newspaper on the table. "The birth certificate says he was born in September and there's an article in the Destiny paper about the Harris marriage in April of that year."

"Ruby, I'm surprised at you judging them for being pregnant before they got married. It's not a crime after all."

"I'm not judging them. And I could be way off base, but what if Jeffrey wasn't Mr. Harris's."

"Then who's child is he?" Violet blinked as the cogs began to click into place. "Ahhh. You think he's Arthur's? That's a huge leap."

"I know, but don't you see how much sense it makes when you think of Arthur's things being stolen and sometimes replaced? Maybe his son wants to reconnect, and Arthur spurned him."

This blew Violet's mind. "If that's true, why would Arthur lie about his relationship with Imogen?"

"He didn't exactly lie, did he? However, not saying that there was something between them does point to him wanting it kept a secret. He could be embarrassed, or is protecting Imogen if she is the thief. It's at least plausible, right?"

Violet stood and paced the library. Up one row of racks and down the other a couple of times. The place wasn't big enough for much more than that, but it was enough to let the idea take hold. "Jeffrey being Arthur's son, makes more sense than anything else I can come up with. She might have decided her son is entitled to everything Arthur has and rather than try to prove the paternity or ask Arthur for anything—she helped herself. The only thing wrong with this scenario is that Linda said Imogen is a sweet person. I wouldn't expect a sweet person to shoot someone in the back."

"Me either," Ruby agreed.

Violet gasped. "The killer couldn't be Imogen, because you saw a man running across the street!"

"That's true. He was wearing a hoodie, so I didn't see his face clearly enough to say who it was, but it was definitely a man."

"What if that man was Jeffrey?"

"It would make sense. The thief had to get hold of the keys without anyone knowing and what better way than via his mom? Frankly, the idea of him stealing from his father is sickening and I can't even deal with what he did to Viktor."

"Me either. The question is, how do we prove any of this is the truth without a DNA report?"

Ruby slowly collected the papers. "You better tell Nate and maybe he can make that happen."

"Maybe you should tell him. He's a little annoyed with me right now."

Cheeks suddenly pink, Ruby straightened. "I can't. Alex doesn't want me to be involved."

Violet was stunned. "Since when does Alex tell you what to do?"

"It's not like that, Vi. He worried that the killer saw me that day at the library and might think I saw who he is. Now he's scared of losing someone else he cares about and thinks we all put ourselves into too much danger. To be honest, he's not wrong, is he?"

"I guess not, but, wow! The giant has it bad for you."

Ruby's eyes twinkled for a moment. "I don't know about that, but he's so sad, I haven't got the heart to upset him more, so I agreed."

"Let me get this straight. You want me to tell Nate about your theory, so you don't upset Alex by doing it yourself even though you're the one who found out all this information?"

"I think in this instance that's best. I'm sure you'll figure out a good way of selling it, because you got to the heart of it right away and you believe it's true."

Violet didn't let the sweet talk fool her. "Like I said, I think it's more likely than anything else and there aren't any clues that we haven't gone over a hundred times. At least the clues we're aware of." That notion actually worried her. Had they overlooked something just as plausible?

Ruby brushed her hands as if she had taken care of a problem or handed it over to her satisfaction. "Let me know what he says."

Violet gave a mock bow. "Just remember that Nate doesn't move at lightning speed if he doesn't think it warrants it."

"Take the paperwork. The proof is all there, to make him want to check it out ASAP."

"There's no way this is solid proof. It's circumstantial at best," Violet reminded her.

With everything neatly folded together Ruby handed her the papers. "I know, but I find that when you deliver facts as paperwork, people often open up and spill the beans, because they think you already know more than you do."

Violet shook her head. "I had no idea you were so sneaky. Maybe pegging you as Ms. Sweet and Perfect has been a gross misrepresentation all along."

"I'm not going to lie—it is hard to live up to the hype."

Ruby giggled and pushed her to the door. "Would you go already and save the day!"

Violet bustled outside to find Deputy Pine backing away from the door.

"I thought I heard you coming. All done?"

"Not quite. Can we go to the café first?"

"I don't see why not."

He seemed far more agreeable now and as they walked down the street in the weak sunshine, Violet felt a little lighter as a plan solidified. And there was one person who might help fill in a few more gaps.

CHAPTER TWENTY-THREE

Outside the cafe Violet held the door open. "It's cold out here. I'm sure the sheriff won't mind you coming inside and having a coffee."

"I like the sound of that," Deputy Pine said affably.

As predicted, with the drama over the craft shop, Olivia was in the kitchen baking, something that settled every Finch woman she'd known.

"How come the deputy is here?" Scarlett asked when Violet went behind the counter.

"It's kinda weird, but Nate has charged him with my care."

"I see."

The tone suggested otherwise and Violet shook her head. "I can assure you it's nothing proprietary. If it was you wandering around town he'd likely have a whole battalion of deputies attached to your apron."

Scarlett snorted. "I don't believe they have battalions in the Sheriff's department."

"Well, I have no idea what a posse of deputies are called, but you get the idea, right?"

"Hmmm. Why do you suddenly sound so chipper?"

Violet casually picked up the mug. "Let me take the deputy his coffee then I'll tell you and Aunt Olivia."

Pine took the mug and thanked Scarlett, closing his eyes at the first sip and Violet grinned. She did make good coffee. Pouring one for herself she went out the back and told Olivia what Linda had said about still wanting the deal to go through. Once that excitement died down, she went onto explain about Ruby's find.

"You must know all about those relationships, Olivia?" Violet fished.

Her aunt frowned. "As much as a person can know when they weren't truly one of them. You must remember that I was a few years older and this was a rather cliquey group."

"But do you think any of it is possible?"

Olivia sprinkled confectioner's sugar over a batch of doughnuts. "Imogen was a shy little thing, but when it came to Arthur, she hung on his every word."

Thoughtfully, Violet stirred a large pot of stewed apples on the stove and pulled it off to cool for the pastry Scarlett was making. The yearbook picture popped up in her mind. "So, what was your take on the dynamics back then?"

"They all knew each other well, though some were closer than others. For example, your dad and Arthur weren't exactly bosom buddies, but you can hardly blame him for that when it was clear how Arthur felt about Lilac."

Violet had a mental image of the two men at war over the petite, fair-headed Lilac Finch. "Did they actually fight over her?"

Olivia snorted. "You do have a vivid imagination, dear. Anyway, not that I recall. Your father simply ignored him for the most part and Arthur certainly didn't go out of his way to get close to him either."

Scarlett wiped her hands on her apron. "What did Mom think of Arthur's crush?"

Olivia touched her chin with a finger. "She thought it was sweet, but I can say positively that she never encouraged him and made it clear where her heart lay."

Violet didn't doubt it. Their mom had never willingly hurt another person and even rude customers were treated with respect. Arthur hadn't spent much time around their family, but once the café was up and running, he'd stop by any chance he could and chat with Lilac for as long as she allowed. From what Violet remembered, her mom had given most customers the same courtesy. That likely annoyed Arthur, especially as he became sick with PTSD which changed his personality so dramatically.

She shook herself. While this trip down memory lane was interesting, she really wanted to hear more about Mrs. Harris. "What did Imogen think about Arthur's fascination with Mom?"

Olivia tutted. "Now, that was hard to witness for everyone, including Jim Harris. She never said a word about it, but her puppy dog eyes were enough to trouble the rest of us."

"But nobody mentioned it?" Scarlett asked.

"What would be the point? You can't help what or who the heart wants, and Arthur simply didn't see her that way. Sadly, Jim was in the same boat."

"Talk about unrequited love. I can't imagine how awkward the whole situation was for the rest of you."

"Yes, it could be awkward, but we had such fun together that I think the ones who were affected by it put up with things and perhaps hung in there hoping things would change."

Violet was curious about that. "And when they stopped hanging out, was it due to animosity?"

Olivia shook her head. "I believe it was simply people moving on with their lives."

"What about you? Did you have a boyfriend?"

Olivia's hands hung in midair over the tray. "I've had one or two, but no one serious."

In fact, the sisters had never seen their aunt in any relationship, which was a little sad and oddly comforting, since Violet had never had a proper boyfriend it was good to see that a person could be happy without a partner. "Did you want children?"

"Of course, but that requires a partner, and I could hardly marry for that reason alone."

"People do."

Olivia sniffed. "Then they are either fortunate to find some happiness or crazy to try."

Violet frowned. "I don't understand."

"You will. In my humble opinion, marriage is for life. Obviously some have to end if one party is unhappy or abusive, but if you don't love a person from the beginning, the chance of it surviving is lessened a great deal."

Scarlett rolled pastry over her pie plates with care. "Hmm. I guess that's true. Although, some arranged marriages end up happy."

"Those are the fortunate ones," Olivia stated wisely.

"Do you think Imogen and her husband were in that camp?"

"I do. They moved away, but I attended the wedding, and they looked happy enough even then."

Scarlett bent to fill the dishwasher with dirty plates. "Is happy enough…enough?"

Violet couldn't see her sister's face, but something in her voice sounded odd. "Are you talking about Imogen being pregnant and maybe having to get married?"

Scarlett bobbed up. "Well, that's what they call a shotgun wedding, right?"

"Are you serious?" Violet scoffed. "They used to, but Jim

and Imogen weren't so young that they couldn't decide for themselves."

Scarlett sniffed. "Did their parents put pressure on them to marry, Olivia?"

"I have no idea. What I can say is that it appeared to be a wonderful day for everyone attending. Now, I must open the craft store for a couple of hours at least. I put a sign up earlier so people would know I was helping out, but I do still need to keep the business running just in case someone does buy it."

Violet nodded as she trimmed the pies, lost in the world of more than two decades ago. She could see her mom wishing the bride and groom all the best, her small hand tucked into their father's—with Arthur watching from a distance. Was it truly a happy time for them all, or were lingering resentments responsible for Arthur's troubles?

The deputy knocked on the counter and roused from her thoughts she went to see what he wanted.

"Apparently Mr. Jacobs is coming back here. I'll go meet him."

"Of course." Though she was feeling buoyed up by all the clues coming together, she would be sorry to see Phin go. And sorry that Olivia had already left.

Hurrying to finish what she was doing and clean up; she was wiping down the counter when the men arrived. Pine hesitated once more at the door.

"I'm sure the sheriff didn't intend for you to watch over us until we closed and I'll go home with my sister."

He tipped his hat. "I'm sure he didn't. Have a good evening and thank you for your company, Mr. Jacobs."

Phin shook his hand and the deputy hurried back toward Arthur's.

Phin had left his overnight bag in the small office area that morning and now went to collect it. "I'm a little sorry to be leaving, despite all the cloak and dagger stuff going on, and I wanted to say how well you're doing, Violet. I don't think you'd be so far advanced if it wasn't for your…experiences."

She smiled, pleased by his comments, and amused by his honesty. "That might be so, but you have a lot to do with how fast I'm learning, Phin. Thank you so much for coming, and I'm sorry that the situation wasn't the best."

"It certainly was different, but it's in the nature of what I do that I often find myself embroiled in scandal or sad tales." He gave a wry grin. "It's a cautionary tale of being careful what jobs you take on and of knowing the people involved as well as you can."

"I never thought of it like that. Like you said, possessions mean a great deal to some people, and I guess passion or devotion can make people do terrible things. I don't like that side of it."

"No one does." He chuckled. "While a little intrigue and a great backstory make the job, the rest can be ugly. Still, I've seen you in action twice now and it seems to me that you have a level head and an inquisitive mind which are the best pedigree for an assessor."

She grinned enjoying the praise. "The only trouble with that is I love all antiques, not just books."

"Knowing what you love is a good thing. You're going to do just fine. Study hard and we'll meet up for a few more sessions before your exams. In fact, I was considering coming to stay for a holiday soon. I hear the resort has had a makeover and I'd love to see more of the town and countryside."

"That would be great. I can show you the sights if you like since you've never really spent much time out of doors either time you've been in Cozy Hollow."

He shifted uncomfortably and looked down the street. "We can talk about that when I see you next."

It sounded as if he didn't want Violet to show him around, which was a little odd. Although, he was a private person and maybe he wanted time to himself to explore. That must be it, she mused.

Unless he preferred anther guide.

She hugged him goodbye, enjoying his pleased surprise at the gesture. "Drive safe."

"And you stay out of trouble as best you can." His answer was not entirely said in jest, and they laughed as he walked to his car.

She stayed to watch him drive down Main Street and was about to go back inside when she noticed Olivia come out of Cozy Crafts. The car slowed and he waved. Olivia waved back—and stayed on the street until he turned the corner.

It was a lucky day when she met Phineas Jacobs. And perhaps not only for Violet.

CHAPTER TWENTY-FOUR

Violet tossed and turned all last night. While Nate might be unhappy with her interference, and there was no proof that Jeffrey was Arthur's son, this might be the connection they were looking for. Still, a little more evidence wouldn't hurt.

Ruby was to help at the cafe this morning and in normal circumstances, Violet was due for a late start. Instead she was feeding the pets after packing the bags of fresh produce.

"You're up early, Vi. What are you doing today?" Ruby asked when she came from the bathroom.

Violet glared at her. "I have errands to run. Is it okay if I use the car today, Scarlett?"

Ruby looked shamefaced as she no doubt recalled the conversation about visiting Imogen. Fortunately, Scarlett didn't picked up on anything as she entered the room groggily.

"As long as you drop me off to the cafe and get you to work in time for the lunch rush. Ruby's taking our unsold food to the drop-off at the church this morning and needs the other car."

Relieved, Violet plucked the keys from the peg by the back door. "No problem, I'll load up the car."

"Do I dare ask where you're going so early since nothing could possibly be open?"

With her fingers around the handle, Violet hesitated. "You can ask."

Scarlett was smiling at George's antics of pushing Bob out of the way of the door, so he'd be first to the car. "I'd like to know in case there's more trouble brewing." Her smile slipped when she caught Violet's eye. "Are you expecting any?"

"Not from me, but as we know that means nothing around here, right?"

Scarlett immediately looked stressed, and Violet instantly regretted trying to make light of the situation.

"Okay, full confession. I'm going to see Imogen Harris."

Scarlett gaped for a moment. "Does Nate know about your visit?"

"Not exactly."

"I suspect you mean not at all. Anyway, I'm glad I asked. Nate told me he's seeing her today, so now you don't need to bother."

Ruby crossed the kitchen to stand between them. "I think she should still go."

Scarlett and Violet stared at her.

"After Violet left me with Linda, I asked her a few more questions in a more conversational way. She was quite candid about their group of friends and how they all adored Mom. She said as soon as Imogen accepted she could never have Arthur, she let the relationship develop with Mr. Harris and they seemed happy together in a short space of time."

"That's pretty much what Olivia said," Scarlett reminded Ruby. "So, it must have been a good marriage and suggests Mr. Harris thought the boy was his."

"But what if it wasn't and Imogen put the idea in her son's head as a way to get Arthur's money. You know he wouldn't say who he was leaving his estate to."

"It's all supposition and none of our business." Scarlett fumed.

"You're probably right," Ruby said gently. "But just in case, I still think Violet should speak to her and find out what she can. I bet Imogen will open up more to another woman, and I think this is what we need to get the case resolved. For Arthur and Alex, who are suffering so much, and for Cozy Hollow so we don't have to live in fear any longer."

Scarlett wrung her hands a couple of times, before finally nodding. "It sounds like you've been doing a lot of thinking and I'm sure anything I say won't change your minds. Only, be warned, I will call Nate as soon as I get to work. I don't like the idea of you going near the place on your own, when we don't know how Imogen is involved and if her son is anywhere near the place. Please be extra careful until Nate arrives, which I'm sure he will do once he knows. And that is the only reason I'm agreeing to it."

Violet nodded. "Don't worry I've already considered everything you've just said, and I hear you about taking care."

"Hah!" Scarlett thrust the float for the register in her bag. "That would be a first."

While Violet could have argued away an hour or two about practicing what her sister preached, she decided to accept that she was getting what she wanted and to keep quiet about it.

They said little on the drive to the café, but Violet saw how Scarlett pleated the bottom of her blouse over and over and felt bad about stressing her out again. "I do promise to be careful," she said as her sister got out of the car.

"You better," Scarlett's voice hitched.

"I love you and Ruby and I'm sorry for being such a pain."

Scarlett leaned in the doorway and gave a half-smile. "I know you are. Unfortunately, I understand the drive behind it. We love you too."

The words ran around in her head as she followed the directions Ruby gleaned from Linda. Slowing as she rounded a corner of the old country lane on the northern side of town she found an overgrown field. A slightly askew letterbox bearing the numbers she sought sat on the edge of a gravel drive next to it. The driveway disappeared disconcertingly to the left behind shrubs and trees.

She sat with the engine idling, suddenly wishing that she'd come with Nate, or perhaps Alex, but they had jobs to do, and she honestly didn't think that Jeffrey Harris would be anywhere near his home right now. Slowly she took her foot off the brake and the car bounced down the dilapidated driveway as she avoided the worst potholes and mounds of displaced dirt.

It was with some relief that she exited the dim tunnel of shabby green and onto a large gravel area in front of a small bungalow. In contrast, the windows shone, and flowers grew healthily in front of the two large windows on either side of the door. As she came to a stop the door opened and a gray-haired woman came out wiping her hands on a worn apron.

Violet slid out from behind the wheel. "Mrs. Harris?"

Lines deepened on the woman's forehead. "Can I help you?"

"I'm Violet Finch."

"Lilac's daughter?" she asked with surprise.

Violet smiled. "One of them."

"Yes, I can see it in your face. You have the same lovely smile."

Since Ruby was the one most like their mom in looks, this warmed Violet's heart. "Thank you."

"I was very sorry to hear of her passing. She was a good

friend when we were younger, but I moved away and lost touch with everyone."

"That is a shame. I heard how close you all were from my aunt."

"Oh, yes. I'd almost forgotten Olivia. She was a little older than most of us, but good fun." Imogen spoke very fast, and her cheeks grew pink. "I imagine that you didn't come here for a social visit on her behalf."

The atmosphere had gone full circle and the woman was wary again."I am sorry to turn up like this, but as you know, Arthur is in danger and he's a friend of the family."

"I imagine he would be."

The sarcasm could only mean that after all these years, Imogen still felt something for Arthur. Maybe Jeffrey had picked up on it too.

"Frankly he's been terrorized. His house has been broken into, burgled and he's been run off the road and forced to flee his property. All this is affecting his health as well as resulting in the death of a good man."

Imogen cowered behind her apron. "I.I.I. didn't know it had gotten that bad."

The pain on the woman's face couldn't be faked and Violet hated that her questions would likely upset her, but she'd come this far and couldn't back down now.

"We both know that Jeffrey wanted to hurt and possibly kill Arthur, and I appreciate that you and he have issues, but no matter why he feels as he does, we must stop him from hurting anyone else."

Imogen took a step back and her hands clenched. "You don't know any of this for a fact, otherwise the sheriff would be here instead. In fact, the sheriff told me there is no proof Jeffrey did any of that, so why are you really here?"

In hind sight, Violet appreciated that her opening gambit was probably a little blunt, but it was too late to take the words back. "Do you honestly believe he isn't the one threatening Arthur and stealing his things? Will you let Arthur die for not knowing he could be a father?"

Imogen clasped her hands to her heaving chest and her eyes filled. "I don't know how it's come to this. He was such a good boy and we loved him dearly. I still do. You can't turn off love just because your child doesn't conform to how you think they should be."

She could see and hear the pain ripping through Imogen, but loving Jeffrey and wishing it wasn't so, wasn't a good enough reason to protect her son. "With all due respect, the death of Viktor isn't anything to do with conforming."

Imogen crumpled to a homemade bench by the door and sobbed into her hands. "Don't you think I know this? If I could change things I would, and if I knew where he was I would tell you. Jeffrey hasn't been home since the last time we fought. I already told the sheriff; my son could be anywhere."

Violet knelt in front of the distraught woman and did the only thing she could. She held Imogen until her sobs lessened. "Shhh. This is not your fault and once we find him he can get Jeffrey the help he needs."

Imogen lifted her head. Hope ran fleetingly crossed her features. "Do you really think the authorities will help him after he killed someone?"

"I do. I'm no expert on mental health, but if he was once as good as you say, then maybe he's had some kind of episode." As soon as the words were out, Violet thought how familiar that scenario sounded.

The hope returned and with it the realization she was still being held by a stranger. Imogen pulled away. "What made you come here? It's not just Arthur, is it? Does this Viktor mean something to you?"

"He's not my boyfriend, or even a close friend, but he is

the best friend of someone I care about. Plus, I care a lot about Arthur. Will you tell me about Jeffrey—how he was and when he changed?"

Imogen's eyes widened for a moment, then her face softened with the slightest of smiles. "Let me show you."

Together they went inside the small pristine bungalow and Imogen insisted Violet sit at the table while she fetched a small case from a cupboard which she placed in front of her.

"Help yourself while I make tea."

Violet flipped the two old clasps and tipped back the lid. Inside were stacks of photos, drawings, certificates, and notes. Most of the photos depicted a boy through the years as he grew into a young adult. There were class, soccer teams, and family photos, all depicting a happy boy and childhood. Still, looks could be deceiving and she took pains to study as many as she could before her host returned.

Imogen placed a teacup and chipped saucer beside the box as well as a handful of separate photos face down, then took a seat opposite.

"These are the more recent ones of my son," she said haltingly.

Violet turned over the first one. The boy was grown into a young man and his face held nothing of promise or happiness that the ones in the box did. Instead, his eyes were hooded. In the next photo he was sullen looking. The rest were similar and yet progressed emphasizing his reluctance to have the photos taken. They were slightly blurred, and he no longer looked at the camera. When she glanced up questioningly, Imogen had more tears in her eyes.

"You see what I mean?"

"I do. It's clear that he was troubled and that it came upon him over a short space of time."

"You're right. You can actually see the life was being

sucked from him. He got very dark, and anything could set him off into a rage."

"Was there one thing, or one time you could pinpoint where it all started?"

"I always said it began sometime after his father died and so I made excuses for his behavior." Imogen shook her head. "To be honest he was moody before then, like a normal teenager is. At least that's what I assumed, but after Jim's death it got steadily worse. That was two years ago."

"Teenagers can be moody, and I can attest that losing a parent is hard," Violet said gently, aware that Jeffrey had left teenage years behind him some time ago.

"That's very kind of you to say, but I don't imagine you did anything too bad."

Violet smiled. "Not to make light of it, but that would depend on who you asked. I was so angry about losing Mom, and angry at having to work in the café, that I'm ashamed to say I acted out and some might say I still do."

Imogen gave a hiccupping laugh. "I heard from my friend and from Arthur how much Lilac loved the café and I've driven by it enough to see how popular it is. She was a fantastic baker when we were at school and won so many awards. It must be hard to follow in her footsteps when you don't feel the same way about it."

That someone who didn't know her could articulate how it affected Violet was amazing and remembering her mom this way made her feel closer to her family. If it wasn't for the terrible situation they found themselves in, she would love to spend more time with Imogen and hear about her mom's exploits and her parent's life before children. Olivia was wonderful, but another perspective was enticing.

"Thank you," she said as she sipped her tea. "When this is over, if you don't mind, could we talk some more about Mom?"

"Of course, and I'd like to thank you for everything you're doing for Arthur."

I Imogen sighed and took her cup and saucer to the small kitchen.

Violet would have liked to ask her more right away, but it seemed Imogen was done with company, so she said her goodbyes and drove away with a small light pushing at the dark edges of Jeffries deeds.

Until she wondered how Imogen knew what Violet was doing for Arthur.

She hurried to Arthur's, desperate to share the information and hear what Nate thought of it. There was still the worry that Jeffrey was nearby and that Imogen had not been as candid as Violet had thought. The pieces were beginning to join and she now had some ideas about how this had started.

CHAPTER TWENTY-FIVE

When she arrived Violet parked on the street and studied the gardens that were so pretty and only now beginning to sprout weeds. Gardens that looked a great deal like Imogen's. Only Imogen didn't have time for all the housework and cooking, so she couldn't have tended the garden. In her mind, another piece clicked into place.

Alex greeted her at the door and put a finger to his lips when she asked for the sheriff.

"Nate said he had something to do but would come by later and Arthur is napping. He's not sleeping well." He whispered and peered over her head. "You shouldn't be roaming the streets."

"I was careful," she promised.

He eyed her skeptically. "If you want to come in and wait for Arthur to wake up or Nate to arrive, I could do with a break to pick up supplies. Ruby mentioned some homeopathic medication that helps with calmness and I thought Arthur could try that."

Violet wavered. Scarlett was expecting her. However she intended to confront Arthur in front of Nate, so waiting for the sheriff seemed the only logical thing to do. "I'd be happy to, if you think he won't mind?"

"Why would he? Arthur trusts you and so does the sheriff." He gave a wry grin. "Mostly. I'll just do a perimeter check, then I'll go."

She shook her head at Alex's teasing, knowing he wasn't wrong, and decided one good turn deserved another. "I see that Ruby is rubbing off on you."

He gave a slight gasp. "I am a perfect gentleman around her."

Along with his pink-cheeks, his horror was cute. "I never doubted it. All I mean is that by spending so much time with my sister, you seem to have adopted her style of teasing."

"Oh. Does any of that bother you?" He asked searchingly.

"I'll let you know when it does."

He frowned until she winked at him.

"I do not always get your sense of humor, Violet, or that of your sisters, but I intend to."

"That is so sweet, but don't underestimate the power of sisters. We have our own language you know?"

When he looked even more confused, she shifted tack. "Where's the deputy who's supposed to be watching the house?"

"He's on an errand for the sheriff, but he'll be back later." With that he shifted into security mode and went outside to do his rounds.

Hopefully Nate wouldn't be too long, because the things she had to discuss couldn't wait. She felt so close to cracking this case and her skin prickled with anticipation.

She watched Alex for a while out the window as he blended into the trees, reappearing every few feet and then gone again. She imagined him doing that over and over since Viktor died. Did he ever get tired of it? Of course, he had been the security guard for the Turner's woodworking factory in Harmony Beach for years. He must know what he was doing and maybe his body was tuned to it, like being on a timer. One the killer might not be aware of, if Alex switched it up like she knew he could.

Arthur's study was the logical place to wait. All the items were put away and the place was tidy once more. She noticed that Phin had left the detailed catalogue they'd made of everything the thief had tried to steal on the top of the desk. It beckoned her. Since she had helped write it, and knew every item as well as Phin did, it was hardly sneaking if she were to study it again.

It had been long, and tiring work cross-referencing the items with their value and history, and though she enjoyed the research, it had little reward except to help Arthur. She sucked in a deep breath, unable to decide if that summed up how she felt because the killer was still out there, or whether she was having second thoughts about her career.

A prickle ran up her spine and down her arms as she checked the list again. That was a shocking idea, and what would she do instead? She pressed her lips together to lock in a moan. If she changed her mind now, after all her fussing, so many people would be let down. And what about her studies? Wasting time and money was never on the agenda for a Finch woman

Violet shook her head and moved away from the desk. These feelings were new and had stolen upon her after Viktor died. Therefore, they must be attributable to any or all of what transpired since. Plus, she was likely being dramatic and oversensitive right now, due to her tiredness from all the mental stimulation, pressure, and fear.

Alex drove by the picture window where sun streamed in and bounced around the room. It hit the old grandfather clock, various photos, and several bottles of what looked like whiskey.

An old-fashioned writing desk that was clearly for show sat in the corner with the top covered in more photos. Violet loved looking at history and these didn't disappoint. There was a sepia one of an older couple, and she suspected these were Arthur's parents. There were several that featured a baby through the milestone of growing up until she could recognize Arthur as a teenager and a young man.

She picked one up for a closer look and sure enough, these did look remarkably like the ones she'd seen of Jeffrey Harris.

There was one more photo that caught her eye. It was of Arthur with his arm around another man—Jim Harris. It was clearly taken around the same time as the year book pictures because their hair and clothes were the same. The two seemed to be comfortable together.

A creak behind her made Violet spin on her heels. The man in the doorway didn't look at all happy to see her.

CHAPTER TWENTY-SIX

"I'm pretty sure Phin said your work is done here."

Arthur's harsh tone was the complete opposite of how he'd treated her before things got so out of hand, and that cemented things in her mind. "It is done, but that's not why I'm here."

"What other business would you want to see me about?"

He'd aimed for a more casual tone, but the tenseness of his jaw was a giveaway. There was no use prolonging this. She took a deep breath. "Arthur, I know who took your things and who killed Viktor."

"I see." Anger turned to anguish and he looked around frantically. "Where's Nate?"

This reaction would be odd, if she didn't know that Arthur was up to his eyeballs in a conflict of interest.

"I haven't told him yet."

Arthur stilled; his eyes boring into hers. "Why not?"

"Because I think it would be best coming from you."

Sweat beaded his brow. "I don't know what you mean by that."

Violet tilted her head. "Yes, you do. You want to protect Jeffrey Harris—in case he is your son."

Arthur clutched his chest and she hurried to his side, helping him to the chair behind the desk.

"Do you really think it's possible?" He gasped.

The confusion in his question tugged at her heart strings. "Oh, Arthur, only you and Mrs. Harris know that."

He gulped. "It is possible. There was a night—it was a mistake and we both knew it right away."

Bearing in mind that it was common knowledge how Imogen felt about Arthur back then, Violet had doubts about the truth of the whole statement. But that wasn't the issue here. "Have you asked Mrs. Harris about Jeffrey's paternity?"

He nodded and dropped his face into his hands, mumbling. "I knew she was pregnant, but never gave the timing a thought. When she'd been working here a while I noticed things about him, before I was aware of anything missing. One day when he wasn't around I finally got the courage to ask. Imogen said probably not, but she didn't know for sure."

Violet bit her lips so she wouldn't comment.

"After things began to escalate with the thieving and Imogen admitted her son had issues. I asked them to leave."

"You talk as though they were both working here? Was Jeffrey your gardener?"

He nodded. "The boy has green thumbs and he was pleasant at first. Imogen begged for another chance, and I felt sorry for her because she needed the money. Though I didn't like the way he talked to her I agreed, and things were okay for a while."

"You mean he stopped taking things?"

"Yes, but as it happened, no. I started to notice the replacements and thought I was going crazy. I had to know and Imogen refused to admit it."

"Was that when she quit?"

He nodded again. "That was one of the reasons. That's why I asked you to help, because I didn't want to accuse anyone—if I was getting sick again and this was all in my mind."

A lump caught in her throat and she swallowed hard. "I think you should start at the beginning," she prompted gently. "And it would be best if you started with how your relationship began."

There was a slight hesitation, then he sat back with a sigh. "As I'm sure you know, we belonged to a large group who were all great friends back then. There was me, Imogen, Lilac, Olivia, your father, Jim, and a few more. When I bumped into Imogen in Destiny a few months ago, it was awkward at first. Because of how we'd parted, we didn't know what to say to each other, but I couldn't ignore her and once we got chatting, something clicked. Suddenly it felt like it had before we made that error in judgement." Raking fingers through his hair, he had a lost look.

"We'd never really spoken about what happened between us, and barely even acknowledged that it had. It was so long ago, that it felt silly to let that interfere with our lives when Imogen needed a job and I need someone I could trust to take care of the house and when she said she had a son who could garden it seemed a perfect solution. I thought we could sweep everything under the rug and carry on as before. Until things started happening."

"Do you mean with things going missing?"

He nodded sadly. "At first I assumed Imogen had cleaned things and misplaced them. One day I made light of it, and she broke down in front of me and asked if I wanted her to leave. It struck me as an over-reaction, and I told her not to worry about it. I let it slide for a while, thinking that I was going loopy."

"Why didn't you call the police right away?"

"Like I said, I thought I was imagining it. Especially when in the beginning things turned up in their place and were close enough to the real thing to make me doubt myself." He looked away. "Plus, I didn't care to see Imogen so upset."

"So, it was her taking them?" Violet ventured.

"Yes. No! Imogen was aware of things disappearing and worried that her son might be involved, so she was the one who tried to replace a couple of items with similar ones. That didn't last long because she couldn't afford to track copies down and pay for them. She begged me not to do anything about it. I was angry and refused. Those things meant a great deal to me, plus the way he'd been so daring and nasty by encouraging me to feel that I was crazy was sickening. I couldn't understand why he hated me so much and Imogen wouldn't elaborate."

He stopped there and helped himself to a small whisky without offering her any before he continued.

"It took a while before she finally broke down and explained that Jeffrey had found a letter from his father. It was mixed up in Jim's possessions after he died and since it was addressed to him, Imogen thought it might be of a personal nature between father and son and would help Jeffrey deal with his loss. According to Imogen, the boy had been having problems for years. he had always suffered from anxiety and depression and couldn't hold down a job. After his father's death he got worse. Unfortunately, she didn't read the letter before Jeffrey, and by the time Jeffrey confronted her about it, he'd been helping himself to things from the house by taking the keys from her purse each evening and then replacing them before she came to work. When I thought about it later, this tied in with why he was always tired."

Violet had a fair idea what came next but had to ask. "What did the letter say?"

"Jim knew he was dying. He wrote to his son that there was a chance he wasn't Jeffery's biological father and that I could be. He stated that Imogen wasn't to blame and that no matter what had happened between me and her back then, he'd always thought of Jeffrey as his."

"So, you agreed not to tell the police about this?"

"I thought it would stop if she wasn't working here and he no longer had access to her keys." Arthur rubbed his face and took another swig of the amber liquid.

"But it didn't," Violet muttered.

"If anything, it made it worse, despite Imogen handing back all her keys."

"You must know by now that he had copies made which gave him total access to the house and everything in it." When he groaned, Violet put a consoling hand on his arm. "What I don't understand is why you let me bring Phin here?"

"I was desperate and felt trapped. I wanted to protect what was left, and if anything happened to me there would be a record of everything including a note about Jeffrey. Besides, it was high time things were properly insured for their worth."

His eyes pleaded for her to understand, but he had put them all in danger and she wasn't sure she could forgive him for that. "Then he killed Viktor."

Tears gathered at the corners of his eyes. "That changed everything. In the short time I knew him, Viktor was courteous and caring. He told me how he and Alex were childhood friends and that Alex had paid to bring him to America out of his own pocket. His plan was to work for Alex and as well as pay him back financially, he would do his best to help build up the diner. After that they would franchise one for Viktor to manage and later purchase. His excitement was what I see in your eyes when you talk about antiques. Or Scarlett's and Lilac's love for the café. And of course, Ruby's love of books. It isn't right Viktor never got to have any of that."

A lump grew in the back of her throat and Violet swallowed hard. "I agree. So why didn't you tell the sheriff right then?"

Arthur lowered his eyes. "I was working on a plan."

"That doesn't sound like a good idea, or that it was working," she noted. "What kind of plan?"

"In his mind, Jeffrey is justified in making make me suffer. Maybe he felt abandoned, and I was wracked with guilt over his struggle with his lineage. I would confront him and if he did want to kill me, perhaps I deserved it, but he would never get away with it."

Violet shook her head in anguish at how low Arthur had fallen. "Letting him kill you and potentially get away is not the way out of this, and why are you talking past tense?"

"I'm so stupid." Arthur groaned and threw the remaining whisky in his glass down his throat. "I left my will and that note I told you about in my safe."

She gasped. "But why would you do that when you knew he could get into it!"

"I'm not talking about the trunk in here. I have a small safe in my bedroom. I guess it's kind of obvious where I put it."

This time Violet groaned. "Don't tell me you had the combination written somewhere?"

He hid behind his hands again and rocked forward, muttering, "So stupid."

He needed a moment to gather himself and so did she.

"I'll make us some tea and together we'll think of a way to sort this mess out."

When he didn't answer, she left him to his anger and frustration, hoping by the time she came back she would have her own under control.

"Poor Arthur," she muttered.

CHAPTER TWENTY-SEVEN

Violet warmed the tea pot with boiling water and scooped in loose tea leaves. Not a big tea drinker, she knew Arthur drank a few cups of strong brew every day and he certainly needed something calming. He had some gorgeous, good quality China. Clearly these weren't something Jeffrey desired enough to steal.

"I see you've made yourself at home."

She spun and dropped the cup which shattered into a million pieces at her feet. As if she'd conjured him out of thin air, there he was the killer. "Jeffrey Harris," she muttered.

His eyes narrowed. "You know who I am?"

"You're Imogen Harris's son."

He gave a mock half-bow. "You always were clever."

This was unexpected and she glanced about her casually. She was several feet from the knife block and there was nothing else to defend herself with, should the ability to do so arise. "You say that like you know me."

"Who doesn't know about the Finch sisters?" He sneered. "Poor little orphans who struck it lucky when they found some old book. The Mayor holds you in high regard based on that alone."

He must have done research on them, which wouldn't be hard in Cozy Hollow. The local paper used any mundane snippet with a hint of promise as the top story, and to be fair the stolen book, plus a subsequent murder, had been anything but ordinary. "Luck played no part in any of that, and it was a terrible time for my family," she told him indignantly.

"You mean it was terrible when it got stolen from your family? Or for the person who owned it and had it stolen first? Either way, you're making me cry."

She ignored his sarcasm. "If you had read all the facts you'll know it was an heirloom and therefore my family didn't steal it, but more importantly, why are you harassing Arthur? Do you want to make him suffer because you think he's your father?"

Jeffrey paled before going bright red. "My real father—excuse me—Jim Harris, believed I was Arthur's love child. He wrote a letter explaining this before he died, so I guess it's more fact than not."

He'd come closer and that, along with his glare, scared her, yet Violet stood her ground. "It is possible, but that's not the same as it being a fact. And even if you are, how is that a reason to kill people?"

"I didn't kill anyone and the letter was clearly a way to make sure I didn't blame my mom over my accidental conception, so her embarrassing past stayed there."

"If he felt that way, why would you try to embarrass her yourself? Don't you care how it makes her feel?"

His face twisted. "Did anyone care about how I would feel? Not that it's any of your business, but I'm tired of being their dirty little secret. They kept it from me all these years and look where it got me!"

He was at the counter now and she arched her back against it. "No one forced you to break the law or kill someone. That decision is all on you." Her hand gripped the teapot like a lifeline, the heat seeping into her knuckles. She had to suck up the pain, it might make a good weapon if required.

"Would you listen! I didn't kill him. I was taking the last load when that monster came after me. I dropped everything and ran to the garage."

The self-loathing that flittered across Jeffrey's features didn't fit with what she knew about him. He was clearly messed up. Was it possible that he wasn't aware of what he was doing when he killed Viktor?

"Why did you go to where the guns are kept if your intention wasn't to harm Viktor?"

"Are you kidding? I needed protection." He huffed. "I had the keys, so it made sense to get a weapon. I just wanted to scare him off so I could get away."

She winced at the plaintiveness. "Instead you killed an innocent man."

"No one's innocent around here!" He yelled. "You're all conspiring to lock me up for taking things that belong to me —or will do, and for things I didn't do. Now, how about you shut up and move over to me, real slow."

She didn't budge. "What could you possibly want with me?"

He licked his lips suggestively. "I could think of a few things, but there isn't enough time."

Her stomach revolted violently, and despite believing he was intentionally provoking her, Violet stayed where she was.

"I said, come here." He waved a gun at her and took a couple of steps toward her.

She nodded at the weapon. "Is that another one of Arthur's?"

"It is. And just in case you were wondering, it's loaded."

Her mouth was dry. Should she keep stalling? He appeared to be at the end of his rope and the belief that someone would arrive to rescue her was dwindling, but she refused to give in. "Someone will be here very soon."

"Giant number 2?" He snorted. "You think he'll come save you? No chance. I heard him say he had an errand to run and watched to make sure he left. It's so hard to get good help, right?"

That smirk on his face was enough to make her fingers itch to slap it away. She never got the chance.

"Put the gun down, Jeffrey." Arthur stood in the doorway, fingers grasping a small pistol.

Casually Jeffrey turned his gun on Arthur. It was a mismatch and Arthur instantly lost any advantage, but there was another thing that drew her attention. Jeffrey's hair at the back was matted with what appeared to be blood.

"Hello, daddy dearest. Have you come to bequeath me all your worldly goods?"

Arthur's hands shook, though his voice was steady. "After everything you've done, I believe you know the answer to that."

"Listening to you two chat earlier, I'd say it was obvious that blood is not thicker than water and getting rid of me is your only plan."

"I'm not some kind of monster," Arthur bellowed. "I'm not the one who kills people."

Jeffrey glared at the gun in Arthur's hand. "You think we're so different? From what I hear you haven't exactly been angelic your entire life. Getting a young girl pregnant and then running out on her is hardly chivalrous."

"That's not how it was," Arthur protested, his face the color of a ripe plum.

"So you say. Mom might want to believe her lies, but we all know the truth. I was an inconvenience when you had such lofty plans that didn't involve a family. To save face, you two somehow tricked Jim Harris into being lumbered with me."

Arthur recoiled. "That's not true!"

Violet saw Jeffrey's trigger finger twitch and had to do something. "If you're so sure Arthur is your father, why not get a DNA test and settle things once and for all? Then everyone gets to move on."

"Hah! You're dreaming if you honestly think you can put a rosy spin on this. As if the police will forget about the dead guy."

"His name is Viktor," Arthur fumed, not helping the situation.

"Whatever. The point is, it doesn't matter one bit what happens now, I'm going to take the fall for your mistakes—whether I add another couple of bodies or not."

He snarled like a trapped animal and Violet could see he was beyond reason. Since Arthur was reluctant to shoot, she had to somehow get the gun from Jeffrey. He was nowhere near the size of Alex, but he was bigger than Violet and probably a good deal stronger. Trying to wrestle it from him wasn't necessarily the best option.

Now that he'd moved away the knife block was a possibility and she sidled toward it an inch at a time. Unfortunately, she hadn't allowed for his peripheral vision which turned out to be very acute.

"Don't be stupid. Knife doesn't beat gun. In fact, nothing does." The smirk suddenly slid from his face and Jeffrey screamed. Something had sailed through the air and struck his arm.

"Knives can beat guns," Alex growled as he covered the distance from the pantry in a few strides and kicked Jeffrey's feet from beneath him. He plucked the gun from the floor where it had been flung.

While Jeffrey squealed like a stuck pig, Alex pulled the man's belt from his waist and slipped it around his upper arm. None too gently Alex fastened the impromptu tourniquet before yanking out the knife. "I missed all your arteries, so stop the wailing."

Still in shock, Violet switched to automatic pilot. Grabbing a small towel she slapped it on the wound, pressing hard to staunch the immediate flow of blood.

"That hurts," Jeffrey moaned.

"You're alive. Be thankful. It's more than you deserve," Alex growled again. "Arthur, call the sheriff."

Bug-eyed, Arthur swallowed several times before retreating to his study.

Slowly Violet's heart calmed to a less frantic beat. "Thank you, Alex. You saved our lives."

Alex looked down to Jeffrey who cowered at his feet and shrugged. "Maybe. I think this pitiful excuse for a man doesn't know what he wants, so it could have gone either way."

Alex never ceased to amaze her and Violet could see why Ruby was so enamored with him. How he'd managed to sneak into the pantry when Jeffrey had clearly been watching them all was a story she wanted to hear. "I'm so glad you didn't wait to find out. What were you doing in the pantry? Jeffrey said he saw you leave."

Now that everyone was safe, Alex's anger dissolved as he made sure they were all okay.

"With the manhunt heating up, I knew he had to come back to confront Arthur today or leave the area for a very long time. Possibly for good. When I saw you arrive from upstairs, I figured he'd be watching and think with me gone you'd never be able to stop him doing what he wanted. Maybe even take you as a hostage."

Some of this made a great deal of sense and yet… "Why would he want me as a hostage when he wants to hurt Arthur?"

"It's common knowledge how Arthur feels about your family. He failed to capture Ruby, but threatening you would hurt Arthur deeper than stealing his property and if he needed to he could use you to get away."

Violet swirled that around for a moment. "I'm not sure that's true. It could be more to do with me getting involved and thwarting his plans."

"It is well known around town that the Finch sisters are good at solving mysteries and I've seen it for myself," he conceded.

"I can hear every word, you know?" Jeffrey grimaced from the floor.

Alex ignored him. "It could be many things mixed together. In a way I think he wanted to be caught, but he's confused and hurting and that made him want to hurt someone else. Perhaps it didn't matter all that much who it was."

"You're wrong," Jeffrey said through gritted teeth. "I'm not confused—it's everyone else with their lies and small town ways."

Alex shook his head. "I don't think so." He glanced toward the back door. "Let's see what the sheriff thinks."

The sound of sirens rent the air and Violet gave a small chuckle. "I thought only Bob and George had an early detection for things like that."

"Where do you think I learned it," Alex said straight-faced.

That's when she saw Bob outside, looking very pleased with himself.

CHAPTER TWENTY-EIGHT

Arthur's house was full of people and Violet watched in fascination as Nate commanded his deputies.

Deputy Pine, so eager to please, forcefully handcuffed Jeffrey, who squealed with pain.

"He's got a cut on his arm you might want to be careful of," she pointed out.

He stared in disbelief and Deputy Glasson took over to escort Jeffrey outside, taking care not to hurt the injured arm.

By manner and tone, the sheriff had been clear he was mad with her, but made sure she was okay and once convinced, took a quick statement from her and Alex, then went about his business as if she weren't there. He took pictures and placed the knife into a bag, while Alex, Violet, and Arthur sat quietly at the kitchen table out of his way.

As the adrenaline left her, Violet took a second to appreciate being safe, and that the case was almost closed. Almost, because something nagged at her. In all honesty it had for a while, but with Jeffrey's continued denial over the killing of Viktor it was now front and center that things didn't completely add up. Sure, Jeffrey could be looking for a way to mitigate the trouble he was in, but he was so adamant.

"Nate, can I have a word?" she asked when he looked like he was finishing up.

"Look Violet, you've done the town a great service, but I'm too busy right now to discuss your part in this any further."

She couldn't make out if he was being sarcastic or not, but she'd never let that stop her before. "I don't think Jeffrey killed Viktor. At least not on purpose."

"That's precisely what a jury is for, so don't worry about it. Deputy Pine can make notes on anything you'd like to add to your statement and then you can go." He curtly dismissed her and walked away.

The deputy pulled out a pad and stood awkwardly nearby as if he was confused about how to proceed. She tamped down her annoyance at Nate's treatment, assuming this was the deputy's first time and waited for him to begin.

He shuffled his feet. "Why did you say that about Mr. Harris not killing anyone?"

"Because someone else did it."

"How do you know that?"

"At the time of Viktor's death, Jeffrey Harris was unconscious," she said louder than necessary.

The deputy hissed out a breath.

Nate's head shot up from several feet away. "What on earth are you talking about?"

Deputy Pine shook his head. "You can't possibly know what happened when you weren't here."

"I know that Jeffrey had a blow to the back of the head and that several times he insisted he didn't kill Viktor."

"Every accused person says they didn't do the crime," the deputy scoffed.

Alex stood. "I also believe he didn't do it."

"Not you too?" Nate grumbled. "Do you have any concrete evidence to support it?"

"I used the secret passage and overheard the entire conversation while I waited for the opportunity to catch Jeffrey off guard and for him to confess. He admitted the theft and harassing Arthur, but denied killing Viktor." He finished with pained look.

Nate glared. "Regardless of what you achieved, that was a risky gamble with Violet's life."

"There was no gamble. This man does not know how to use a gun."

"How can you say that?"

"I was close enough to see that the safety was on, and I heard enough to form my opinion. Plus there are other things that don't fit. Aren't there Violet?"

It was as if he were giving her the opportunity that Nate wouldn't and Violet stood beside him. "Jeffrey could have taken everything in a couple of days and been far away if stealing from Arthur was truly what he wanted. He also could have killed him a dozen times, including while he slept."

The deputy snorted. "That's because he wanted to torment the Mayor for not accepting him as his son."

Violet raised an eyebrow. "That's true, Deputy. At least that's the conclusion the rest of us came to and I guess it's common knowledge at the department that Jeffrey could be Arthur's son, right Nate?"

Nate stared at her. "No, it's not."

"Oh. Then no one else would know that this was even a possibility, unless they knew Mrs. Harris or the mayor really well. Although, since they never spoke of it in public, that would be difficult to accept, right Arthur?"

The mayor sat up straighter at the kitchen table. "We told no one."

Violet looked to Nate who nodded for her to continue. "Of course there is one other way for someone to know."

"What way?" Pine demanded.

"The safe upstairs. In it Arthur placed a note documenting everything, from his friendship with the Harris's, to the possibility of him having a son and who that might be."

"Then it's clear cut," the Deputy stated. "Jeffrey had all the keys, so he obviously got into the safe behind the picture."

"Except that it had no key and the combination was on his laptop which was also broken into, and where a password file sits on Arthur's desktop."

Deputy Pine paled. "You seem to know an awful lot about what's in the file."

"More importantly, how do you know there's a safe in Arthur's bedroom?" Violet paused for a plot second. "I don't believe anyone mentioned that."

He licked his lips nervously. "I saw it when I was doing the walk through after the first incident with the light upstairs."

The sheriff moved forward to stand in front of him. "I recall that you weren't in the house that night. In fact, you were charged with guarding the perimeter."

"Then it must have been another time. I was there a lot."

"Yes, you were."

"Are you accusing me of something, Nate?"

"Right now, I'm the sheriff and I'm charging you with the murder of Viktor Petrov."

Pine backed away, eyes darting left and right. "That's ridiculous."

"Take your hand off your holster!" Nate yelled.

But Pine wasn't listening. His fingers expertly slipped the gun free of the unclasped holster and lifted it toward the sheriff.

For the second time, a knife flew through the air to find a

specific target. The gun fell to the floor and Pine grasped his hand with a squeal. Before anyone could say or do anything more, words spewed out of his mouth.

"You have to understand, it was an accident. I was in the corner of the garage by the gun safe when Jeffrey ran in. I didn't want him to know I was there, so I sneaked up on him and knocked him out with the butt of a rifle. Then suddenly Viktor was there and I was trapped."

"And your only option was to kill him?" Arthur asked grimly.

"I told the fool to stop, but he kept coming like a train, so I aimed the gun and he turned tail. I followed a way to ensure he wouldn't attack me as I left. Just as I was about to run, he reached the veranda and the idiot pulled a knife from his boot." Deputy Pine blanched. "It was supposed to be a warning shot."

"Aren't you supposed to be a crack shot?"

"Why don't you just mind your own business!" he screamed at Violet.

Alex took a step toward the deputy who cowered.

"I think we've heard enough for the time being." Nate handed Alex his gun and cuffed Pine, then retrieved both guns. "I'll take him to the office and see you all there when you're ready."

EPILOGUE

Violet sat back on the Victorian armchair and made room for a huffy George who felt this space was his and that it was a huge imposition for him to share it. "Well, I'm glad that's all over. Apart from the court case."

Nate nodded. "They take a while to get through the system, so none of you should dwell on it too much."

He was speaking more to Arthur, who was still haggard-looking, but Nate's gaze ended at Scarlett. A born worrier, she'd been out of sorts during the whole sorry business. Violet thought she knew why. Her sister's sense of responsibility to Violet and Ruby was so acute, she considered it a personal failure every time one of them got into trouble. The problem was, the three of them couldn't let people suffer, or go it alone when a crime arose. As much as Violet would like to promise Scarlett she wouldn't dig into anymore dramas, she couldn't. Just as they couldn't promise her.

"You knew it was Deputy Pine, didn't you?" Arthur asked, oblivious to the undercurrent.

"Not from the start," Violet admitted. "Once we figured

out that copying a set of keys was the only logical answer for the criminal, Imogen was top of the list. You made it easy to eventually discount her by vouching for her so strongly, and I'm certain that she didn't want to be involved."

"The poor woman," Olivia tutted. "Being frightened of her son that way is awful."

"She certainly didn't deserve to be treated so badly." Arthur looked a little sheepish. "I hope the police will look at the big picture, Nate."

"I can't make any promises." Nate shrugged. "She should have told you immediately the keys went missing, or come to me. The courts will take a dim view of that as it makes her an accessory—whether she was a willing one or not."

"I know what you're saying is true, but people do things under duress that they wouldn't normally when they can't see another way out of it." Arthur sighed deeply. "At least I'll be able to sleep at night knowing the killer is behind bars. While Imogen and Jeffrey won't get off scott free, it is tragic how their situation evolved. It's just a tragedy that Viktor died because of greed and ignorance. I'd rather not have my possessions if it would have prevented all of that."

"I agree about how tragic this is and I feel that Jeffrey's mental health needs looking into," Violet added.

"Tell us again how you figured out it was the deputy who killed Viktor," Scarlett demanded.

"I know it's easy to say now, but he bugged me from the start." Violet shrugged. "I couldn't put my finger on it, and to be honest I didn't try too hard, because of Imogen and Jeffrey."

Nate squirmed in his chair. "I guess we all learned a lesson from that and I'm sorry I gave you such a hard time."

"I'm sure some of it was justified," Scarlett told him. "Go on, Vi."

"Charming. Well, he slipped up a few times with where he said he was and where he actually was. Then there was knowing things that he shouldn't have along with the whereabouts of the safe. He was using Jeffrey as the scapegoat for stealing and also by giving him the ability to access Arthur's house over and over again during the investigation."

"Did he need the money?" Ruby interrupted.

"I overheard him tell Phin that his mom ran the family farm and she needed his wages, so I guess so. At the same time, Pine also said he was a crack shot, so when he told us he had only intended to fire a warning shot at Viktor, that's when I was certain."

Alex shifted from his perch on a kitchen chair beside Ruby, which looked about to give way. "Jail is too good for Deputy Pine."

Violet nodded. "He was an opportunist, and I'm glad he won't ever have another opportunity to represent the law. Jeffrey's case is much different. He's unhinged to believe he had a claim to everything of Arthur's and made no attempt to discover the truth, but something you said rings true, Alex."

"What is that?"

"He didn't know what he wanted and that made him desperate. He couldn't hold down a job and being fired by Arthur must have notched his angst up to a breaking point."

Ruby sighed. "Before that, I imagine after finding out his father potentially wasn't who he thought, and not able to process things properly, he felt adrift. He needed to feel that he belonged somewhere and perhaps having things from his ancestors around him would give him that."

Ruby's way of thinking often made sense, but by the way Alex looked down at his rough hands, he didn't seem convinced.

Arthur rubbed his fingers through his hair in agitation.

"Since I don't have any family of my own, that does resonate with me. The stupid thing is, if he'd come to me before all this nonsense, I would have welcomed him with open arms and considered giving him something that might have helped." Arthur shook his head sadly. "I don't know exactly what, but I couldn't do that now after everything he's done."

"You might change your mind once he's done his time," Ruby gently suggested.

Arthur looked away and Violet didn't like Jeffrey's chances, but as she knew, there was always room for hope and people could change. Arthur was a classic example of this. And, when she thought about it, the Finch sisters had also changed in many ways since their mom passed away. They were still a close family, and she hoped they would always remain so, but they were finding their own way in life and the happiness that brought about showed and could not be underestimated. Jeffrey hadn't understood that his mom deserved his love and respect, and no one owed him a darn thing—least of all Arthur.

Bob dropped his large head into Arthur's lap and gave him a doe-eyed stare. Obediently, Arthur scratched between his ears. "I swear this dog knows what's going on and he's telling me things will be okay."

Ruby laughed. "George has taught him a lot, but Bob also has a natural empathy for man and beast alike."

"Just like you," Alex said softly.

"That is so sweet," Ruby patted his arm. "Which is just like you."

He blushed and ducked his head. A big man, with strong feelings, Alex had a tender heart and it seemed Ruby liked that side of him a great deal. Obviously she would take pains to ease Alex's sorrow and perhaps with time help him get over his hatred for Pine. And that was no small thing.

Scarlett and Violet grinned at each other. It looked like their baby sister was hatching her own story and Violet was pretty sure it would have a happy ending.

Of course, there were no guarantees in a place like Cozy Hollow, where things were not always as they seemed.

THANK YOU

Thanks so much for reading Berry Betrayal, the fourth book in the Cozy Cafe Mysteries series. I hope you enjoyed it!

If you did…
1 Help other people find this book by leaving a review.

2 Sign up for my new release e-mail, so you can find out about the next book as soon as it's available and pick up a bonus epilogue. If you've previously joined my newsletter, don't worry, you'll be able to get it very soon for free and many others.

3 Come like my Facebook page.

4 Visit my website caphipps.com to see all my books.

5 Keep reading for an excerpt from Book 1 - Beagles Love Cupcake Crimes, from the Beagle Diner Cozy Mysteries.

BEAGLES LOVE CUPCAKE CRIMES

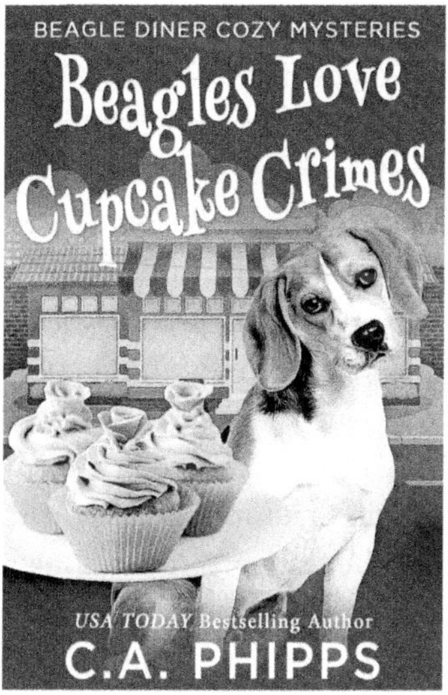

Cinnamon waited at the door with wet paws. Lyra followed her prints and two other drier sets of human shoe prints to the main bathroom, which was full of steam.

Dan moved back from the doorway, as did Maggie who pointed in horror at the new mirror.

Lyra frowned, then sloshed through an inch of water which had been prevented from seeping into the hallway by a mountain of towels, to where words were scrawled diagonally across the glass in condensation. Now that the hot water was turned off and the window opened, the words were fading and a couple of letters had disappeared, but it was still readable.

You don't belong here!

A shiver ran up Lyra's back. "What the heck is this about?"

"I've got no idea." Dan pointed to a sodden towel at his feet. "Whoever turned the tap on placed a towel along the door so that the water would back up. It's not too bad considering I don't know how long the tap was running, but we'll have to wait for the floor to dry out completely before the tiles go down. That will set us back a few days."

His practicality almost made her smile. Solving another mystery so soon after the last shambles was not on Lyra's plan, and it made her angry. "I don't care so much about that. The note and towel mean this was done deliberately, and I want to know why this person wants me gone. Plus, how did someone get in here without you or Cinnamon noticing?"

Dan dipped his head. "Cinnamon looked bored over by the diner, and I hadn't had my lunch, so I took her and my sandwich down by the stream. I didn't think to lock up."

He looked so miserable that Lyra forced herself to take a deep breath. "This is not your fault. We've all become lax because this isn't LA or Portland and no one seems to take security too seriously around here."

"But you're not just anyone," Maggie pointed out. "You have fans who take liberties. They won't all disappear because you're no longer hosting a show. There is cable you know, and reruns worldwide."

"You don't seriously think a fan has followed me here?" The shiver from before reached her voice.

"Anything is possible, but that's only one scenario." Maggie attempted to reassure her. "There was a lot of drama around you buying the diner because the conglomerate wanted the whole main street knocked down and remodeled. Plus, there were those who were worried that you would bring big-city ways to town. Or maybe it's someone who wanted the diner for something else."

Lyra clenched her hands. "No matter the reason, I won't be run out of town. We need to find this troublemaker before they do something else."

"I'd like to point out that it could be a one-off," Dan suggested hopefully.

"Perhaps." Lyra liked his optimism, but she couldn't let things get out of hand the way they had in Portland and LA when she hadn't followed up hard enough after several crimes. "Meanwhile, let's make sure the house and diner are locked up if no one's there. I'll head over to the police station and tell them what happened in case they want to see the mirror or check for fingerprints around the house."

Cinnamon decided to tag along, but they were hardly down the steps when the beagle stopped. Nose twitching, she turned away from Lyra and disappeared around the side of the house. Lyra hesitated; she still had pies to fill after visiting the police, but her dog was clearly on a mission. Cinnamon sniffed around underneath the bathroom, then looked up and barked.

"What is it, girl?"

The beagle sat and lifted her right paw, still looking up. There was a slight slope leading down to the stream, and a small tree sat close to the window. From one of the branches hung a hat. Lyra stretched up on her tippy toes and yanked it free.

Fairview Forever was emblazoned on the rim. "I've seen these around, Cin. Do you think the person who broke in and left the taps on dropped this?"

The beagle wagged her tail and looked up again as Dan poked his head out the open window.

"I thought I heard you talking." He smirked.

"Look what Cinnamon found on that shrub." Lyra waved the hat at him. "Did you leave the bathroom window open when you were out?"

He blinked. "Now that you mention it, I thought I had, but it was closed when I got back."

"Hmmm. That implies that the person either went in or came out the window," Lyra mused. "Maybe both. Perhaps while they were trying to close the window, they lost the hat."

Maggie joined Dan at the window and leaned on the sash. "That makes sense because there were no wet footprints inside the house other than ours. They had to have left this way unless they didn't wait for the sink to overflow."

"The hot water had to run a while to fog the mirror, and the window would need to be closed." Lyra paced around the tree. "Can you see there are a couple of broken branches at the top? They have to be strong enough to hold their weight, so it can't be a small person."

"Although, those branches aren't terribly thick," Maggie noted.

"You reached the hat," Dan pointed out. "Which means the person must be shorter than you."

"True, but maybe they heard you arrive, were in a hurry to get away, and simply didn't have time to collect the hat."

Rob McKenna poked his head around the corner. "Seems like a funny place to have a party."

"No party; it's more of a brainstorm," Lyra explained. "Somebody broke into the house and turned a tap on. The bathroom was flooded, but Dan caught it in time before it spread through the rest of the house."

"Well done, lad. That could have been nasty after all your hard work. Any ideas on the culprit?"

"None, but they left this hat hanging on a shrub." Lyra held it out to him.

"It looks pretty worn, but I'm sorry to say that most residents have one of them, including me." Rob shrugged. "Seems to me that it could have been left by anyone at any time."

"Really?" Lyra twisted the hat in her hands. "That's a shame. I thought it was a great clue."

"Sorry to burst your bubble. The town committee got a bunch of them made up when we had a fishing competition a while ago. It was back when we were being proactive about getting tourists and some new residents."

"You mean that not only people from Fairview might have one of these caps?"

"Unfortunately, that's likely true."

"Darn it." Lyra sighed. "I thought we might be onto something."

"Well, if anyone says they lost their cap, I'll let you know," Rob said, deadpan.

He loved to tease, and this wasn't such a big deal, but what if it heralded the beginning of something worse? While she wasn't naturally pessimistic, recent history had slightly scarred her optimism about such things. "I guess the likelihood of that happening is remote. Since it's not life-or-death, we haven't rung the police, but I'm going to the station to report this."

"I'll come with you," he offered. "Sheriff Walker can be hard to talk to."

Lyra didn't doubt that. The times he came in for coffee or a bite he had stared far too much for her liking. He was good-looking with short brown hair which made his cool gray eyes even more startling. And piercing. She got the impression he didn't know what to make of her and she felt the same about him.

"In that case, I'll be glad of the company." She looked up to find Dan and Maggie gazing at each other. "Could you two clean up the water, but leave the mirror and keep Cinnamon here?"

It could have been the sun warming their faces, but both were pink-cheeked.

"Leave it to us," Dan called, then moved back into the room.

The station wasn't far. They crossed the street at the end of Lyra's drive, went up the road, and passed a couple of houses. When they got to the corner, they crossed again. The station was five doors down, and Rob explained that it was usually manned by three police officers. Also, the sheriff had towns to the east and west that he oversaw, so he wasn't always there.

The few times she'd seen him in the street, or when he'd stopped by for coffee, he'd given her a penetrating look that was both embarrassing and annoying. Naturally he would have heard rumors about her troubled past and quite possibly investigated them. Which should have exonerated her from anything that he could dig up. Whatever his reason for being less than friendly, she didn't like it one bit.

"I hope this isn't our designated walk for today. Even if you have provided a little more drama than usual," Rob teased.

"You can't get out of it that easily. Besides, Cinnamon won't be happy that we've left her behind."

He nodded. "She does like her freedom."

Rob opened the door for Lyra, and inside they found the desk clerk reading a romance novel. Her badge read Officer

Moore, and when she noticed them, she quickly stuffed the book under the counter.

"Ms. St. Claire, what can I do for you?" she gushed.

Lyra had seen this kind of reaction so many times it hardly affected her, and she quickly explained the situation. When she finished, the clerk blinked several times before responding.

"Goodness, that's a tricky one. With almost everyone owning a hat like that, I don't know how we can say who did this."

Lyra breathed deeply. "Officer Moore, I appreciate that right now we can't pin it on anyone, and the writing on the mirror will be gone," Belatedly, it occurred to her that she should have taken a photo, "but is there a chance that someone could come take a look at the crime scene?"

The officer shot a longing glance at where she'd stowed the book. "I guess it couldn't hurt. Let me speak to the sheriff."

Lyra sighed as the woman disappeared out the back and took a seat on a hard wooden bench. "We might be here a while."

"It could be worse." Rob dropped the words enigmatically and sat beside her.

They waited for ten minutes, scanning all the brochures on display, until the sheriff appeared. Tall and roughly Dan's build, his hair was pressed down on top as if he'd recently worn a hat. He ran those cool gray eyes over Lyra, then grimaced at Rob.

"Officer Moore told me about your problem, Ms. St. Claire. It seems a little far-fetched that someone would break in to cause a flood. Are you sure that your handyman didn't leave the tap on?"

His dismissive attitude rankled, and it was an effort to be polite. "Thank you for seeing us. I understand that it's not much to go on, but if Dan had done that, he would have told me so. And why would he leave a note on the mirror telling me I didn't belong here when he lives in my house? Also, I know he doesn't have a cap like this." Lyra handed it to him.

The sheriff turned it over a couple of times in an unconcerned manner. "While it's commendable that you trust your handyman, it just doesn't seem like something that would happen around here. Maybe Dan would prefer to get back to the big city sooner than you thought. Now that the major building has been completed, an ex-army man probably has a few more abilities other than doing odd jobs. As for the cap, I'm sure Rob told you they're a dime a dozen and could have been left there by anyone before you showed up—or after."

Lyra stiffened at the mention of Dan wanting more than working for her. It sounded as though the sheriff had been doing some checks on the town's newest inhabitants and made a few judgements. "I can assure you that Dan is free to leave whenever he chooses and has no need to make up ridiculous scenarios to do so. Finding out why that cap was stuck in a tree outside my bathroom would be a better question?"

He shrugged. "It gets windy around town. I dare say it blew there."

"Since I've been in Fairview, it hasn't been windy at all."

Sheriff Walker narrowed his eyes as if she'd called him a liar. "Lucky for you. Now, if you're done, I need to get back to solving real crimes for our residents."

Irritated by his dismissal, Lyra noted he kept the cap.

"Thanks for dropping by. I do love your food, and your show was amazing," Officer Moore gushed. "It's such a shame that you lost it."

Lyra simply nodded as they left. People couldn't appreciate that she was happy to give up her fame for a diner in

Fairview. "How about that? He wasn't the slightest bit interested," she told Rob when they got outside the door.

"I confess that I was curious if you'd have more sway with Walker than me. Since he was giving me the side-eye, I decided to keep my mouth shut, but it seems he treats most people with the same disdain."

"I guess a flood isn't high on a priority list. We were lucky that Dan found it when he did."

"Don't you fret. As much as it doesn't seem like it, the sheriff doesn't like drama in his towns, so he won't sit by and do nothing, and I'll keep an eye on the house."

The sheriff's style of working was certainly interesting, but she wasn't satisfied with the outcome. "Even if we all took turns, it's not possible to watch it all day. We have businesses to run, and Dan and Maggie are busy too."

"I take on less work these days, so I have time to wander by. I'll make it known around town that there was a break-in. If someone's worried about getting caught, they won't like that, and the rest of us will be more vigilant."

"Thanks for the help, but last thing I want is for you to put yourself in danger."

"A person who turns on a tap isn't likely bent on physically hurting another." Rob scratched the top of his head. "In my opinion, your tap-turner is a coward."

"I hope you're right. Please be careful, and call Dan if you see anything. Now, I better get my pies done, the pastry will be ruined and I'll have to start over."

About to part company at the corner, Rob raised an eyebrow. "We can't have that. Perhaps I better check one to make sure they're okay before you try to sell any."

Lyra groaned. "Another tester—just what I need. Come by in an hour, and they'll be ready."

"No need to twist my arm." He waved and swaggered

toward his garage, several doors down the street from their houses.

One of the unforeseen pleasures of coming home to Fairview was her next-door neighbor always made her laugh.

NEED to know what happens next? Get your copy of Book 1 in the Beagle Diner Cozy Mystery Series, Beagles Love Cupcake Crimes now!

RECIPES

These recipes are ones I use all the time and have come down the generations from my mum, grandmother, and some I have adapted from other recipes. Also, I now have my husband's grandmother's recipe book. Exciting! I'll be bringing some of them to life very soon.

Just a wee reminder, that I am a New Zealander. Occasionally I may have missed converting into ounces and pounds for my American readers.

My apologies for that, and please let me know—if you do try them—how they turn out.

Cheryl x

STRAWBERRY AND CREAM CHEESE MUFFINS

Ingredients:

2 cups self-raising flour
½ cup castor sugar
1 egg
¾ cup milk
1 tsp vanilla essence
3 ½ 0zs / 100 g butter
1 tbsp golden syrup
12 tsp raspberry jam
12 tsp cream cheese
Confectioners' sugar for dusting

Instructions:

1. Heat oven to 220C / 428F and grease 12 medium muffin pans.
2 Sift flour into a bowl and add sugar. Stir.
3 Beat egg and add milk, vanilla essence, golden syrup and melted butter. Stir.
4 Pour wet mixture into dry mixture and combine with a spatula until smooth.

5 Spoon into pans to halfway. In the center add a tsp of cream cheese and then drop a tsp of jam over that. Cover evenly with remaining mixture.
6 Bake for 12 minutes and cool before dusting with confectioners' sugar.

COCONUT AND MAPLE SYRUP COOKIES

Ingredients:

3 ½ 0zs / 100 g butter
1 tbsp maple syrup
1 tsp vanilla essence
¾ cup oats
¾ cup flour
¾ cup coconut
½ cup sugar
1 tsp baking soda dissolved in 1tbsp hot water

Instructions:

1. Heat oven to 180C / 350F and line a tray with baking paper.
2 Melt butter, vanilla essence and syrup in a saucepan, then cool.
3 Mix rolled oats, coconut and flour with the sugar.
4 Stir dry mixture into wet mixture in the saucepan until smooth.
5 Dissolve soda in water and add to mixture.

6 Drop ½ tbsp per cookie onto baking tray and flatten slightly with a floured fork.
7 Bake for 12 minutes or until brown.

ALSO BY C. A. PHIPPS

The Cozy Café Mysteries

Sweet Saboteur

Candy Corruption

Mocha Mayhem

Berry Betrayal

The Maple Lane Cozy Mysteries

Sugar and Sliced - Maple Lane Prequel

Apple Pie and Arsenic

Bagels and Blackmail

Cookies and Chaos

Doughnuts and Disaster

Eclairs and Extortion

Fudge and Frenemies

Gingerbread and Gunshots

Beagle Diner Cozy Mysteries

Beagles Love Cupcake Crimes

Beagles Love Steak Secrets

Beagles Love Muffin But Murder

Please note: these are all available in paperback.

Remember to join Cheryl's Cozy Mystery newsletter.

There's a free recipe book waiting for you. ;-)

ABOUT THE AUTHOR

'Life is a mystery. Let's follow the clues together.'

C. A. Phipps is a USA Today best-selling author from beautiful New Zealand. Cheryl lives in a quiet suburb with her wonderful husband, whom she married the moment she left school (yes, they were high school sweethearts). With three married children and seven grandchildren to keep her busy when she's not writing, there is just enough space for a crazy mixed breed dog who stole her heart! She loves family times, baking, rambling walks, and her quest for the perfect latte.

Check out her website http://caphipps.com

facebook.com/authorcaphipps
twitter.com/CherylAPhipps
instagram.com/caphippsauthor

Printed in Great Britain
by Amazon

25442685R00138